CW01648543

The Scream

by Ruth Calder Murphy
with Mathew Taylor

www.ruthmathews.net

Published in 2012 by FeedARead.com Publishing –
Arts Council funded

A CIP catalogue record for this title is available from the British Library.

"We all share not just a sense that there is such a thing as justice, but actually a passion for it, a deep longing that things should be put to rights, a sense of out-of-jointness that goes on nagging and gnawing and sometimes screaming at us…"

N. T. Wright

Chapter 1

At first, there was only darkness - a long tunnel of impenetrable gloom. Then, a gradually intensifying light that first crept then rushed then all of a sudden flooded in upon me. I woke up.

My journey began somewhere between the beginning and the end. All journeys do; this is nothing new. Now that I am in a place where I can rest and breathe and my memory is recovered so that I am able to see all the pieces of the puzzle and how they fit together, I have a strong urge to set it out clearly, in order - exactly as it happened - so that people might as it were accompany me on my journey. So come with me if you will to that day - a grey day, neither warm nor cold; a nothing day when everything started.

The first thing of which I was aware was the movement of the train. I registered this and as I did so, opened my eyes. Perhaps aided by the sudden return of sight, all my other senses simultaneously burst into life. At first, all I knew was that I was bumping and swaying along in a small room of sorts, a large, brown, labelled case beside my feet and muted greens and greys flashing past the noisily rattling windows. There was a cocktail of smells on the air - coal smoke, cigarette smoke, stale sweat and dust. They stuck to my tongue and tickled my nose. I sneezed. As my senses had awakened with the opening of my eyes, so with my sneeze words and ideas began to slouch into my mind like truants caught scrumping apples and brought late to class. They looked shifty as though they would rather be anywhere but here in my head. They would not catch my inner eye and it took a great deal of firmness and to be honest a few thrashings before they settled down and began to feel at home. 'Train'. That was the first word. On its reluctant heels followed 'journey', 'luggage' and finally, slinking in behind the rest and I think hoping to slip by unnoticed, 'myself'. With this latest addition to my little class came a sense of unease - a chill in my belly that communicated first with my legs, setting them to spring me out of my seat, and then with my brain that gazed out of the window at the blurred landscape.

"Who am I?" My whisper was hardly there at all over the thunder of the train. "Who am I?" I said louder and it was as though my voice was waking up from a long sleep. It sounded unfamiliar and startling and I looked over my shoulder to make sure that I was still alone. As I did so, my glance caught the label on my suitcase. I could see that it had writing on it and I stooped to turn it so that I could read what it said. The writing was clear, bold, a sloping, well-formed hand. "Sam Roden," it declared mutely, staring up at me like an accusation. "Sam Roden," I replied meekly. And so I was. At least, I knew nothing of being anybody else, so Sam Roden I would be. I straightened up once more and breathed deeply of the stale air. I had a name. Stolen or given I did not know, but a name nevertheless that I would own. It made me feel stronger somehow, more real. "Sam Roden," I said again. "I am Sam Roden." I sat back down on my seat, one foot resting on the suitcase. I suddenly felt very proprietorial. The suitcase must stay safe, attached to me. The suitcase was my Evidence. The label continued to stare. I smiled at it. It looked right through me. I shrugged and lay my head against the high back of the seat. I felt the coarse fabric scratch the skin of my neck. I closed my eyes, my foot still on the suitcase and slept.

I woke to the sort of commotion that can only be caused by a train under full steam coming into a station. Whistling, hissing, the screeching of wheels and brakes, shouts, hollers and the banging of doors. I sat up, surveyed the inside of my head and did a quick check. All present and correct. 'train', 'journey', 'luggage'... I looked down at the label. It had turned its back on me. I felt a blunt stab of apprehension in my abdomen as I bent down and turned it.

"Sam Roden," it maintained, bored by now. My stomach lay back down and I breathed again. 'Myself'. I nodded to the class to carry on. I looked out of the window. There were not many people on the platform. A guard, two passengers who were already making their way out of the station and a scruffy looking dog who sniffed and barked at them as though he was fulfilling a contract. I was about to settle back in my seat when the door of my compartment opened and a man wearing uniform and impressive facial hair put his head around it. He nodded genially enough and said, "All change sir." I looked at him. I felt startled.

"I'm sorry?" I said, rather stupidly I am afraid.

"Why? What have you done sir?" said the guard, throwing me momentarily into a state of confusion. His face was dead pan and his tone flat. Seeing my discomfort, he relented and chuckled. "Just joking sir," he said then he had to stop as his chuckling caught on the coal dust and he coughed and spluttered for a moment. When he had finished, he said, "All change sir. End of the line."

"Sorry," I repeated, feeling more stupid by the minute. "Do you mean I have to get off here?"

"Quite right sir," the guard replied, "Quite right. End of the line see. Nowhere else to go."

I hesitated a moment and then said, "But I don't know where I'm going..." The guard came fully into the compartment now and his voice became a little impatient as he reiterated his case.

"Here," he said after he had done so. "Let me help you with your luggage." I suspect he was trying to chivvy me along and who could blame him? I also noted the omission of his customary 'sir' when addressing me. I realised that I had no choice in the matter and thanked him somewhat dejectedly. He carried my suitcase off the train and placed it gently but decisively on the platform. Then, checking to make sure that I was really off the train, he trudged into the guards' lounge. Once the door had shut behind him, I was alone on the deserted platform. The light was beginning to fade to a twilight thinness and for the first time I felt a slight chill. I shivered and from somewhere in my broken memory a phrase slithered through my head.

"Someone walked over my grave," I muttered to myself. And with that cheery thought I picked up my suitcase and began to walk as purposefully as I could to wherever my feet would take me. As I left the station I realised that I had not even looked to see where I was. I turned back to look for a sign. There was none, unless the rumble of thunder in the distance can be counted as such. I shivered again and started to walk.

Chapter 2

I did not have far to go before my feet informed me that I had arrived at 'wherever'. I looked to see where it was. I had been walking along a straight road with a pavement accompanying it on each side. Across the road on my right, beyond the pavement was a wall then a sandy beach and beyond that the grey line of the sea. I noticed with interest how these words appeared in my mind as I saw the objects to which they related as though they had been there all along but only upon seeing the beach, the sea, the pavement, the road, was the light turned on so that I could read their names. The salt breeze rolled over me like the breakers from which it came and I found I did not enjoy the sensation. I turned my back on it and looked to my left. A stately line of tall, red brick houses stood there, looking out to sea like stern aunts who disapproved of one getting one's feet wet. I wondered where the metaphor had sprung from. I was certain that a moment before I would not have known what an aunt was nor what sternness might be. But there it was. It was as though I was being fed certain thoughts and denied others, for when I turned my thoughts inward to focus on what was there, I was presented with a profound darkness which if it contained anything at all, obscured its contents entirely from my questioning gaze. This made me squirm more than the sea breeze had done. To change the subject of my thoughts, I looked more carefully at the houses and knew straight away which one I was to approach. A sign swung and rattled at the foot of the five steps that led up to the door. 'B&B' it stated. I did not know what this meant but I did not need to know. This was the place to which my feet had brought me. This was the door on which I needed to knock. I knocked, twilight deepening around me, my case precarious on the top step, my right knee braced to stop it tumbling, the rest of my body thrown forwards to prevent the same thing happening to myself. In this position my hostess - a statuesque, handsome lady only very slightly shorter than myself with neatly coiffed brown hair and large dark eyes - found me when she opened the door.

Her surprised expression gave me to think that she was used to greater dignity in her guests, but she was apparently a woman of impeccable manners and good breeding as she rallied immediately and held the door open for me to enter. I instinctively removed my hat and entered the house with a word of thanks and what I hoped was an appropriate smile. She looked at me, returning the smile and assessing my face as though it were a character reference. I hoped it passed. I caught a glimpse of it in the large mirror on the hall wall and decided that it was a face I could live with; presumably I had already lived with it adequately enough. It was a strong, oval face topped with sand coloured hair. Blue eyes reflected back at me and a smile still hovered around the mouth. My mouth, I should say. My hostess smiled more assuredly now and I relaxed a little, taking this as my certificate of approval.

"Good evening Mr…?" she said, her intonation clearly demanding a name with which to address me.

"Roden," I said slightly awkwardly. It felt like wearing a new hat for the first time - a mixture of pride and self consciousness and an illogical need for approval. "Sam Roden." My hostess relaxed a little. I reflected briefly on the positive effect of knowing a name, whether one's own or one's acquaintance's.

"Mrs Downing," she reciprocated. "Elizabeth Downing." She began to turn towards the stairs, presumably to take me to a room, but then she paused. "Are you here visiting family?" she asked.

"No," I said, uncertainly. I felt suddenly insecure. My suitcase had said nothing about family.

"I've got three brothers and two sisters," Mrs Downing continued. "I sometimes feel as though I can't get away from them. What about yourself?"

"Myself?" I stammered. What about myself? I felt as though I might lose consciousness. The world suddenly seemed very precarious. I thought of my suitcase on the top step and pictured myself tumbling, tumbling...

"Have you brothers or sisters?" Mrs Downing's voice brought me back to the moment and I blinked.

"No," I said. "At least, I don't know. I don't remember." I felt miserable. I must have sounded miserable too. I repeated my name to myself in the recesses of my mind. *Sam Roden, Sam Roden...* It worked. I felt stronger again, strong enough to weather her raised eyebrows.

"You can't remember if you have brothers or sisters?" she said, understandably incredulous. I slumped. I decided to come clean.

"I can't remember anything," I said. She looked at me for a moment, a slow, appraising look. Her face registered a procession of responses before she spoke, none of which I felt confident to read.

"Have you taken a knock to the head or something?" she asked, her voice concerned. She looked at me again, then apparently coming to a decision, walked around me and, myself watching her in the mirror, examined the back of my head, first with her eyes and then, gently but purposefully, with her fingers.

"I don't think so," I mumbled indistinctly, but as I said it I realised that for someone with no memory whatsoever, my not thinking so was meagre evidence either way. Mrs Downing completed her examination and returned to face me.

"I can't find any evidence of a knock," she said. "Come with me. I'll show you to a room and you can rest. Perhaps you will feel better once you have eaten and slept." With this she turned and began to climb the stairs which led back towards the front of the house and onto a landing. As I followed her around the top few stairs, a large window reminded me where I was. The beach was shrouded in dusk now, but I could still make out the darker line of the sea. In fact, it had drawn nearer in the time it had taken for me to come this far. My hostess noticed where I looked.

"The tide's coming in," she said. "And it's looking choppy tonight." She continued across the landing, past three closed doors to a second flight of stairs. As she turned onto it, she added, "A night to stay inside I'd say." I looked up at her and our eyes met. She looked quickly away and began to sweep up the stairs.

Carrying my case I was slower to reach the upper landing and arrived a little out of breath behind her. As she selected a key from the chain at her waist and fitted it to the lock, I had a sudden startling premonition that I knew what was beyond the door. A picture of the room came into my head, complete and in life-like detail. A floral wallpaper, chintz and lace, a pink room with a picture window that looked out to sea. I could see the bed, dating to the middle of last century, the bedside table, the dressing table and the wardrobe, all crystal clear... She pushed open the door. The papered walls were painted white with blues and greens detailing the woodwork. Chintzy curtains, but also blue and green, no pink and the picture window looked out onto darkness. The furniture was new - strikingly so. I blinked and frowned. The room was not the room I had imagined. Mrs Downing looked at me. I must have swayed because she reached out and touched my arm.

"Here, why don't you sit down for a minute?" She took my elbow and guided me to a chair. Then she brought my suitcase into the room and put it out of the way. She looked at the label just as I had done. "Sam Roden," she confirmed. She looked at me.

"I think so," I replied. "That's what it says on my case." I paused, doubt oozing like blood from under a bandage. "That is, if it really is my case." She looked at me a moment longer.

"You really are in a bad way aren't you," she said.

A little while later, after I had washed and unpacked and to my extreme relief had discovered that the clothes in the case were my size and that everything I needed was in there, but disappointed that there was nothing amongst them that might give me a clue as to my identity, I went back down the two flights of stairs to the lounge. There I discovered my hostess busying herself with straightening some ornaments. On a whim, perhaps remembering my inaccurate premonition on entering my room, I said, "Excuse me for asking, but do you know me? Have I been here before?"

"I don't think so," she said, glancing briefly at me over her shoulder. "We do have a lot of guests... I suppose it's possible. Would you like to look through the guest book?" I hesitated a moment and before I could answer she had indicated a large, red, leather-bound book on a table beside the picture window - a larger version of the one in my bedroom - that looked out to sea. I sat down at the table, noting as I did so a calendar upon it that informed me that it was Wednesday, 5th October 1949, and began to flick through the pages of the book. There were hundreds of names and I soon became despondent and decided to give it up for the evening. I felt suddenly claustrophobic and despite the lateness of the hour, decided to go for a walk. I rose to leave and Mrs Downing turned around to acknowledge my movement.

"Did you find anything?" she said.

"No," I replied.

"So..." It was her turn to hesitate. "So," she repeated and this time, frowning slightly, she continued, "You don't know who you are, where you're from, where you're going or what you're doing here?" I looked from her to the window, where night brushed against the pane behind reflected lights and our two indistinct faces. She crossed the room and pulled the curtains snugly across the glass. I waited until she had finished and had turned back to me before replying.

"That's right," I said. She nodded. I suppose there was little to say. "I think I might take a walk," I said. "Along the sea front perhaps."

She nodded again and this time said, "That's right Mr Roden. Clear your head a little. Will you require supper this evening?"

"Supper?" I repeated foolishly.

"Yes. I can do a light supper for you if you wish. Cold meats, cheese, bread and cake, perhaps some cocoa."

"Ah," I responded as another light came on in my brain, "Yes please, that would be good."

"Very well, I shall leave it in your room at about eight o'clock."

"Thank you," I said.

"And breakfast is also at eight o'clock," she said. "In the morning," she added, wisely covering the possibility that I might not remember that there was a difference.

"Thank you," I said again and made my way back up the stairs to my room where I put on my overcoat and hat, picked up the keys that had been left on the bedside table and went out, locking the door of my room behind me.

I did not intend to walk for long, but the air was bracing and this time I found that I enjoyed it, coming as it did out of the darkness. I felt an empathy with the night where usually familiar things were obscured, where one might come upon another person quite unexpectedly, in the same way that my thoughts sidled out of the shadows of my mind. I have no idea how long I had been walking when out of the darkness there came a sound, shrill as nails scraping down a slate. A scream that carried on the night air like ice and left the darkness torn in such a way that I supposed demons might use the rent as a portal. This childish supposition twisted, more firmly than it had any right to do, into my tired mind and I decided to linger no longer but to head for the warmth and security of what I supposed I must call 'home' in the absence of any other. I looked around, wondering which direction to take and saw that I had almost come full circle and was only a few minutes' walk from where I had begun. Those few minutes took me, almost running now to the door of my room and into the quiet, chintzy nest where supper awaited my return. I ate and drank what I found there then, having placed my tray on the landing outside my door, I performed my ablutions and climbed into bed. I remember nothing after my head hit the pillow until I awoke some long time later.

Chapter 3

When I awoke I had almost as little idea of time and place as I had possessed in those first conscious moments on the train. I sat up in bed, pulling the bedspread up around me as I did so, not for warmth so much as for something to hold onto. I looked around the bedroom and my first thought was that I had been ill and had slept for several days. I had no evidence for this beyond my own unreliable senses and yet the feeling persisted as I climbed out of bed and began to prepare myself to face the day. I checked the time on my pocket watch, which informed me that it was half past seven. I assumed that it was morning.

My memory may have been lacking but my body seemed to know how to dress itself appropriately and I went downstairs wearing my clothes as they were intended to be worn. I walked down the short hallway and approached the breakfast room. As I was about to reach it my progress was arrested by my hostess who greeted me with raised eyebrows and a small smile.

"Good morning Mr Roden," she said. "I am pleased that you feel able to join us for breakfast." I tried to decide whether her tone implied that I had missed other breakfasts between my last supper and this morning's meal, but she continued to speak and I really could not be certain either way. "There is another guest staying with us since last night," she was saying. "A gentleman. He asked me to invite you to sit with him at breakfast. I believe he wishes to speak with you."

For a moment I felt confused, but as my thoughts arranged themselves, my hopes began to rise. As Mrs Downing turned away from me and towards the back of the house from whence emanated smells of cooking food, I hastily asked, “With me? Did he... Does he..." I hesitated but realising that my hostess was impatient to return to her kitchen, I ploughed on. "Does he know me? Does he know who I am?" Her answer put my hopes back to sleep.

"No," she replied. "I think not. He merely wanted to talk to you. He talks," she said in the tone of someone who has experienced the fact first hand, "to anyone." With this, she bustled away and I was left hovering outside the breakfast room door, unable to see around it, my curiosity vying with an illogical apprehension. As I stood trying to pluck up the courage to enter the room, a voice called to me. It was an accented voice. Although with my memory as it was I could not place it, I did recognise that the intonation was different from that of the other people I had spoken with.

"Mr Roden?" It called. "Mr Roden? Won't you please come and join me?" I paused as I registered embarrassment at having been caught procrastinating and tried to send messages to my feet to oblige me by walking into the room, thus saving me more of the same. "I have coffee," the voice added and there was a new tone there. Another word, another light coming on in my mind. I was being teased. As I came to this realisation, my feet finally gave in to my demands and carried me through the door.

It was a light, high ceilinged room overlooking a long, well tended garden. A concreted area, decorated tastefully with potted plants, led to steps which in turn led onto a well-groomed lawn with herbaceous borders. A wall and a trellis arch over which roses and clematis climbed, divided the garden in two and beyond it I thought I could make out vegetable plots and fruit trees. The room itself was readied for breakfast with six smallish tables and two chairs at each. There was also an armchair in the corner by the window, turned slightly so that its occupant when it had one - for now it was empty - might look out and enjoy the serenity of the garden. At the table in the furthest corner from the door and facing it, sat the only other person in the room. He held a newspaper in front of him but was not reading it at the moment because he was looking at me. He was dark haired, more swarthy skinned than myself, and wore a well groomed moustache. He smiled but did not stand.

"Ah, Sam Roden. Good morning." He indicated the chair opposite himself. "Won't you please sit down?"

"Thank you," I replied and did so.

"May I pour you some coffee?" he asked. I was not at all certain what flavour coffee might have nor whether I would like it, but this was the second time he had mentioned it and with some enthusiasm in his tone. I accepted. He took a moment to pour, during which I tried to catch the fragrance of the dark liquid. It was not a difficult thing to achieve. The aroma rose easily and filled my head like morning. I smiled and he caught my look and smiled back. "It is good, yes," he said. "Elizabeth she has told me of your unfortunate lack of memory. Well," he gestured to the steaming cup, "introduce this to your little grey cells and if they do not sit up and tell you all, well they will at least be happy with you." He nodded encouragingly as I took a sip and allowed the taste to travel over my tongue. It was bitter, but combined with the fragrance of it became somehow wonderfully smooth before it reached my throat when sure enough, it hit the front of my brain like ammonia. I returned his smile.

"It is good," I said and the gratification on my companion's face made me feel as though I had passed the first test. Just then, Mrs Downing returned with two plates of cooked breakfast.

"Mr Pierre," she said, placing one of them in front of my new acquaintance and helpfully informing me of his name.

"Please," he corrected her. "Just Pierre. We will not stand on ceremony so early in the morning. Thank you Elizabeth," he added, deliberately. Again that word. Teasing. He was teasing her, I thought. He looked at me. "I have requested Elizabeth that she bring the same for you," he explained as the second plate was placed on my side of the table. "I considered that if you had no memory, it would be all the same to you to try anything at all. See? Eggs, bacon, sausage, tomatoes, the fried bread... The full English breakfast as they say."

"Thank you," I said, addressing both my hostess and my eccentric companion.

"You are welcome Mr Roden," she replied. Again my companion protested.

"Please please," he said. "We are living here together. Tutoyer. Let us be friendly with each other." He nodded at me encouragingly.

"Sam," I said obediently. "Please, call me Sam." She hesitated and then a little laugh, short and involuntary, escaped her. I could not tell then what provoked it. Nervousness, amusement, a slight discomfort I could not have said.

"Elizabeth." She shook her head just very slightly and left the room.

"Well," said Pierre, beginning to eat. "So this is nice, is it not? The two of us here, eating breakfast, the peaceful garden, the tick tock of the clock." I listened. He was right. It was tick tocking and from the garden I caught the trill of a bird. I said nothing. I was not sure what to say so took a mouthful of food instead. We ate in silence for a few minutes and then, "I wanted to talk to you," he took a sip of coffee, "about the thing that has happened here."

"The thing?" I paused, a forkful of bacon halfway to my mouth.

"The thing," he confirmed solemnly. He wiped his moustache with his napkin then he brightened and seemed to change the subject. "You went for a walk did you not? By the sea front."

"Yes," I replied, slightly puzzled. "Yes, then I came back to my room and had supper." I paused, wondering whether to ask him how long ago this had been. But before I had an opportunity, he was speaking again.

"And why did you come back when you did?" he asked. His tone was not confrontational, but it was probing. I tried to remember. There was a mist in my mind but all of a sudden it cleared and I remembered.

"I heard..." I paused. What had I heard? That noise, that sound. "I heard a scream," I said as the light came on. "It sounded like..." Again I hesitated. What? What had it sounded like? I did not need to wait for the light to reveal the word. Instead the word switched on the light.

"Like someone being killed?" Pierre finished for me, his tone rising questioningly. Killed. With the light came a darkness and an abyss opened up before me. New words - death, dying, killing, dead - spewed from the abyss and blackened my brain. When I recovered some awareness of other things, I realised that Pierre was looking at me keenly. "What is it?" he asked. "What is it when I say 'like someone being killed' that makes you pale?" He was leaning forward and looking intently into my face. I realised that I was shaking.

"I..." I took a deep breath. I felt as though the air had become thin. "I had forgotten about death." My tongue was dry and my voice felt thick. I took a mouthful of coffee and felt a little better for it. My companion leaned back in his chair, his fingers resting lightly on the edge of the table in front of him. His eyes never left my face.

"Interesting," he said. "Yes... And yet..." He paused, perhaps waiting to make sure that I was listening. "*Someone has been killed*," he continued when he had ascertained this. "Someone is dead." He sat up again and began to eat. I wondered what he meant. Someone killed? Recently? He seemed to read my mind. "Recently, he said. Yes. Someone was killed." My mind reeled.

"So the scream..." He said nothing. I supposed he felt it was unnecessary. He continued to eat and I played with my food for a moment. "Who..?" I suddenly felt an overwhelming need to know. "Who?" I said, more urgently. "Who was it?" He looked at me and again I felt as though he was searching my face.

"Elizabeth's daughter," he said softly. "Mary." I looked at him. Again that sense of reeling - a sort of internal vertigo.

"Mary?" I echoed.

"Yes. She was nineteen." He sipped his coffee.

"Is she... Mrs Downing... Elizabeth..." I paused. "Is she... She seems..."

"She seems to be coping surprisingly well?" He raised one eyebrow in a question.

"Well, yes. Is she alright?"

"No," he replied. "Of course she is not alright. But people have different ways of being alright. Or not alright as the case may be. Now," he said suddenly brisk. "We must finish our pleasant little déjeuner and make as they say 'tracks'."

"Tracks?" I echoed. I wondered whether he thought me very dull for my parrot impressions. He seemed not to notice.

"We must go into the village and ask questions," he continued decisively. "We have much to learn."

"We... We do?" I stammered.

"We do," he confirmed. "You will come with me, yes? I need to have your eyes, your ears, your wonderfully empty memory." Here he beamed at me, throwing me into mild confusion. "It is a perfect receptacle," he added, "for new ideas." He paused. "Or old ideas," he corrected himself thoughtfully, "with a new perspective." With this, he became brisk again. "I will meet you in the lounge in five minutes."

Meekly, I obeyed and went to my room to don overcoat and hat. After all, I had nothing better to do.

Chapter 4

It was exactly five minutes later when I arrived in the lounge. Pierre was already there waiting for me. He was standing beside the table on which the guest book was kept, staring out of the window. He did not turn round when I entered the room but continued silently, as he had been before. I began to feel a little awkward and considered giving a cough or some other such indication of my presence, but just as I was coming to the conclusion that this was the best course of action, he spoke and I realised that he had known all along that I was there.

"The sea, it is so wonderfully vast is it not?" I followed his gaze to where foam was being flung over the sea wall from the lively breakers. I considered his statement. To be honest, my mind was still full of the vastness of death and the enormity of killing. The vastness of the sea seemed somewhat diminished beside them.

"It is finite though," I replied and as I said it the concept of infinity joined my Class of Ideas under the light. I shuddered. Pierre looked at me curiously.

"Yes..." he mused. "Yes, it is finite." He turned and smiled at me. "It is also a bit stormy this morning. I wonder if we might have some rough weather in store." He crossed the room to the door and I followed. "Let us make those tracks about which we have talked," he said, his tone lively. "We have questions to be asking."

We walked down the road along the sea front. The day was grey and the sky lowered so that it skimmed the tops of the cliffs with its frown. The tall, smart terraced houses continued in blocks for perhaps a quarter of a mile until the road was forced by a high, rugged, grass-topped cliff, to turn away from the sea. Gulls called as they rode the rapid air and the grass on the cliff lay flat under the force of the sea breeze.

The foot of the cliff was almost within reach and I could see the road curving away to the left, when Pierre stopped outside one of the houses. I looked at it. It was similar in appearance to the houses on either side of it, but like our own guest house announced itself with a swinging sign.

"Police."

Pierre pushed open the gate and led the way along the short path to the front door. The road rose gradually from the station end to this, and to keep the houses level with each other, the number of steps up to the doors had diminished in accordance with the gradient of the road, until at this, the penultimate house, there was only one step. Pierre rang the impressively strident bell and while we waited for a response, I looked at the house. I realised that in fact, although it had once certainly been two houses, now it had been made into one, making the police station the last house, not the penultimate house as I had thought, in the row. As I was lazily turning these things around in my mind, I became aware of footsteps approaching from the other side of the door and tried to pull my thoughts together. I found this to be no easy task, having no context from which to draw them and was relieved when Pierre stepped forward to address the opener of the door, who proved to be a middle aged policeman, in full but slightly disheveled uniform; as though he had put it on in a freshly pressed state but had then gone to bed and spent the night in it. He peered at us, his eyes squinting a little - from short sightedness or suspicion I could not say.

"Yes?" he barked gruffly, after a slight pause, during which he wiped his mouth with a handkerchief which looked as though it, too had spent the night in less than favourable circumstances.

"Good morning, Sergeant Griswold," Pierre said with a disarmingly bright smile. I looked at Sergeant Griswold's face. He did not look so much 'disarmed' as 'on guard'. He said nothing. Pierre continued. "I am Pierre Massenger and this is my assistant, Sam Roden. I wonder if we might come in for a few minutes."

Sergeant Griswold continued to stare at us then, with no variation in expression and no response other than a mumbled grunt which may have been words but if so I could not make them out, stepped aside and indicated with a wag of his hand that we should come in. We did so and found ourselves in a narrow hallway not dissimilar to the one at the guest house. The stairs, leading up from the hall, had a rope across them with the word 'private' hanging from its centre. From somewhere above us wafted the smell of bacon. It occurred to me that we had probably interrupted the sergeant's breakfast and I glanced at Pierre to see whether he had had the same thought and whether it made him feel awkward, as I confess it had made me. From his benign expression, I could not tell whether the idea had occurred to him, but I was fairly reassured that he did not feel awkwardness of any kind, for any reason. Sergeant Griswold shut the door behind us and there followed an awkward few moments during which he manoeuvred his ample frame between us and the wall in order to take the lead. This done, he grunted again and began to walk towards the back of the house. Pierre, unperturbed by the sergeant's rather ungracious manners, bounced jauntily after him and I, rather more perturbed, followed.

The sergeant led the way to the end of the hallway where, as in the guest house, a door led through to the back of the house. The other doors along the hall, which in the guest house were the sitting room and the breakfast room, were labelled 'Waiting room' and 'No entry', respectively. The door through which we were led opened into a long office that in turn led onto other rooms. The sergeant settled himself behind an immense desk that was piled with papers amongst which nestled a telephone like a black egg in a white nest. He shuffled some of the papers importantly before looking at us and saying, still in the same brusque tone, "Take a seat."

There were two low armchairs placed opposite him and we did as we were told. Once seated, it felt as though our heads barely rose to the level of the paper-strewn surface and the sergeant, mounted on his own far higher chair, his elbows planted firmly on the desk and his hands locked together above them, became somehow more formidable in an instant. He glowered at us. I risked another glance at Pierre. The same benevolent expression lingered on his face and he too had his hands clasped together, his left elbow on the arm of his chair, his right index finger to his lips. He returned the policeman's unblinking stare with an amiable smile. I was not surprised that it was sergeant Griswold who looked away first. However I wished it might have been otherwise, because finding Pierre imperturbable, he turned his stare towards me. I think I pleased him by immediately looking down at my knees. At any rate, he gave a little 'harrumph' that sounded almost approving. Having thus satisfied his pride, he turned back to Pierre.

"Questions, you said."

"Indeed," Pierre replied. "Questions about law and order and a recent lack of it on occasion." He nodded, still holding the policeman's gaze.

"Law and order you say?" responded the sergeant, puffing out his chest a little. "Well then you've come to the right place. What is it you need to know?"

"It is about murder," said Pierre. "The murder of Mary Downing in fact. Can you help me with this?"

I wondered whether the sergeant's chest might explode, he puffed it out so much as he replied, "Well I should hope so! This is a police station after all. What about it? Are you friends of the young lady? Do you have information for me?"

"Perhaps I could help you," Pierre said rather vaguely, "But it is not to give information that I came but to find out the facts of the matter." The policeman narrowed his eyes again and deflated to a more normal size.

"And you are?" he said.

"As I said already, I am Pierre Massenger and this is..."

"Yes, yes, you did say that. I mean, in what capacity are you asking for this information? We don't give things out to any old Tom, Dick or Harry you know." The chest was expanding again and I looked across at Pierre, hoping that he would say something soothing. He did not disappoint me.

"No, no of course you do not," he said. "You are the very epitome of professional policing, Sergeant Griswold. I merely wish to learn from you a few facts. I am investigating the matter privately. I will not be an obstruction to you I promise. I have come here first because of course this is the place where I will learn the facts. This is, as you say, The Hub of the investigation.

The professional centre of activity. I have come to observe the masters of law and order in action."

Sergeant Griswold relaxed a little and preened. I thought I even spotted a smile lurking somewhere behind his expression as he nodded and blinked and said, "In that case, my man, you have certainly come to the right place. I will tell you whatever you need to know, as long," here he paused and raised his eyebrows and his index finger importantly, "as long," he repeated "as it does not compromise my professional duties." Pierre nodded solemnly.

"But of course, I understand," he said. "Me, I am also a professional person. I know this is important. So," he beamed at the policeman, "Can you tell me please what happened to Miss Downing?" The sergeant took a deep breath and blew it out as an introduction to his reply.

"Well," he said. "It's a terrible thing of course, a young lady like that going out as she was to see her friends, all innocent and pretty and not a care in the world but there you have it. Lawless, some people are. No fear of God in them. No fear of the law neither and that's where I come in. I," he said, his chest inflating so much that it pressed against the edge of the desk and moved his chair backwards a fraction with an audible creak, "I put that fear into them." Pierre nodded again.

"So you have caught this perpetrator?" he said, "You have put this fear into him?" The sergeant sagged a little.

"Not as such," he said. "No. Not yet. But we shall. We shall and then..."

"I'm sure you will get to the bottom of it," Pierre said soothingly then added, "So what happened? You know this of course."

"Oh yes, yes of course," the policeman blustered. "She was attacked in the alleyway. Strangled. Her mother found her you know and informed us."

"And the murderer?"

"Got clean away," the policeman said. "A bad lot for sure. Clean away and not a trace of him." He shook his head and then said, "But we'll get 'im. You can be sure of that. Justice will be done, you can be sure of that."

"Yes, yes. You are right of course. Justice must always be done. And her mother? She was very distressed, yes?"

"Oh yes, well you can imagine. She's a strong lady, Mrs Downing. No fainting or any such silliness with her," he said with a trace of admiration, I thought. "But it was her daughter you know, got killed. I would say she was upset. Angry too. As well she might be."

"And she came straight to you," Pierre said. "After she found her daughter's body?"

"Well of course she did," the sergeant exclaimed. "Where else would she go?"

"And did you go with her? To see her daughter's body in the alleyway?"

"Well no," replied the policeman. "You see, she had her daughter with her. She carried her here you see. Strong woman as I say. Strong woman."

"And then you went to look at the alleyway? For clues?" Pierre pressed.

"It was dark then. We went as soon as it was light. No point looking in the dark you see."

Pierre got to his feet. "Thank you very much for your time sergeant. We will not keep you from your important work any longer. Nor indeed from your hard earned breakfast." The sergeant also got to his feet and walked around the desk. He held the door open for us and followed us out into the hallway. I wondered whether we would be required to perform for a second time the uncomfortable door-opening choreography in the cramped hallway. However at that moment, the door opened from the outside and a slightly younger, rosy cheeked policeman stepped through it. He smiled openly at us.

"Good morning!" he said brightly. "I see business is off to an early start here today, Sergeant Griswold."

"Yes, Inspector Miles," he replied, a note of resentment creeping into his voice. "We are kept busy." Unlike the Sergeant, Inspector Miles was brisk, nimble and lean. He turned easily out of the way of the door and allowed us to pass him and step out of the building without pulling our breakfast-laden stomachs in. He smiled again and we bid the two policemen good bye.

As soon as the door shut behind us, I felt the bullying of the wind again and did not even attempt to speak as we turned out of the gate and back onto the pavement. Pierre followed the road around the foot of the cliff and as we moved behind it and were protected from the wind, we were able to walk more comfortably and to hear each other speak without so much effort.

"How did you find the sergeant?" he asked, as soon as he was able. I hesitated. I was not in the least sure that my findings would be in any way valuable. But Pierre was waiting for an answer and so I gave one.

"I think he was reluctant to leave his breakfast," I said. Pierre laughed.

"Yes, I think you are right. And he was reluctant to be visited so early by his superior law keeper also." Pierre chuckled.

"He didn't seem..." I paused, searching for a way to phrase what I was thinking. "He didn't seem very disturbed by the fact of the," I hesitated again. The concept and the word itself were still profoundly distasteful and somehow alien to me. I swallowed. Then, "the murder," I finished. Pierre looked at me and nodded, but said nothing. I realised that he was waiting for me to elaborate. "He seemed more concerned with being seen to be in control than with the fact that a life has been taken."

"Yes," said Pierre. "I think you are right. He is quite proud that one. But I have seen prouder. I think he is not hard. He is just, how do you say? He has the tunnel vision. He sees the job and he wants to do it. He wants to be seen to be the one to do it." Pierre sighed. "Unfortunately, the tunnel means that he cannot see very much at all. Still. These people, this is what we are looking at. All these people will speak to us in the way they react to this terrible thing. It is not just their words, Sam. It is their priorities we must watch." He looked at me. "We will speak with all different kinds of people. See now this morning, we will talk to some of them."

"Where are we going?" I asked.

"A good question," Pierre replied. "A very good question. And the simple answer is, we are going first to the big house you see up ahead." I looked where he indicated. There was only one house he could mean. It was a large white house with a gravel drive and by the look of it, gardens to the side and the back. Over the high garden wall I could see trees and climbing plants. I had a sudden longing to see beyond the wall into the garden, but instead we walked up to the imposing front door and Pierre pulled the bell cord. We waited a few moments then heard brisk footsteps emanating from the back of the house and approaching rapidly.

The door was opened by a formidable looking lady of middle age, who glowered at us. Despite her diminutive stature - her head did not quite reach my shoulder - my first thought was that I would not like to cross her. Her eyes met first Pierre's, who stood closest to the door, and then my own, the gaze of which I confess I lowered immediately. In fact it was this lowering of my gaze that meant that I missed the softening of the person who caused it. I was startled, an instant after my eyes registered the awkward scuffling of my foot, to hear a melodious female voice say softly, "Oh I'm sorry sir... Sirs... I thought you were someone else. Why it's every half hour some days, those children. Ringing the bell and running away. And I know it's child's play sir and I don't want to be a dragon, sure I don't. But what they don't seem to understand, them and their playing, is that some of us have jobs to do and not enough time to do 'em in."

Here, the woman, whom I confess I *had* rather assumed to be a dragon, chuckled and I realised that she really had rather a pleasant face when wreathed in laughter. At this point she seemed to remember herself and the fact that one of her jobs was opening the door and responding appropriately to whomsoever might be standing there. She now seemed quite relaxed and I was struck again at how in fact she was actually quite attractive when she wasn't scowling. I realised, with a little discomfort, how easily my interpretations of people and what they were or were not like, depended on what they were prepared to reveal to me. If a simple and involuntary change of expression could make so much difference to my perception, how far could I be misled if that was a person's aim? The thought did not have long to settle because the woman was speaking again.

"Anyway sirs," she said, her tone taking on a more business-like quality. "What can I do for you?"

I was very glad that it was Pierre and not I who had the task of introducing us and our business. I still felt hampered by my lack of memory and did not feel qualified to say the right things at the right times. In fact, I realised that I simply did not know what or when those things and times might be. I had no need to consider this however, as Pierre made up for my ineptitude with his own capability.

"Good morning madam," he was saying. "I am Pierre Massenger. We are here, my assistant Sam Roden and myself, to ask some questions. You know of this unfortunate incident..." He did not name the incident but I saw the woman's expression change to one of indulgent grief and she clicked her tongue several times, shaking her head to the rhythm of it, before replying.

"Oh a terrible thing sir, a terrible thing. Such a lovely girl and so young and pretty she were too. And you know of course as she was going to be married to the master's boy, though not so much of a boy now, James. A fine young man in fact though between you and me she would have needed to have learned him a thing or two about putting his boots tidy in the evening. But there! Listen to me! As if you was wanting to know that sort of thing sir. Please, come in. So you are investigating Miss Mary's... The tragedy then. Oh such a pity. Such a terrible thing sir."

By the time she had arrived at this last utterance, we had arrived with her in the large, fashionable drawing room at the front of the house. The walls were painted ivory in the modern way, not papered, and the seats were upholstered in dark red to match a beautiful carpet on the floor. Dark wood beams contrasted pleasantly with the cream walls and a large window at the front of the house let in sunlight whilst another smaller one to the side gave me coveted glimpses of the gardens. We sat at her invitation and she busied herself for a moment, setting a light to the ready laid fire in the grate.

"A comfortable room," my companion said when there had been enough of a pause in the woman's outpourings to render his own observation timely. "Very pleasant. You keep a well ordered house, er..?"

"Sophia sir," she said, straightening and turning to face us again. "Thank you sir. I do my best to be sure. The master - that's Mr Beresford sir - he appreciates a tidy house. 'A place for everything and everything in its place' that's his motto and between you and me, he'd do well to inform Master James of it. Everyone toes the line - all of us in our places if you will sir - but young James, oh I love the boy don't get me wrong but he always was a bit of a lacksadaisy if you get my meaning. Still he'd have made a fine husband for Mary he would. A bit of responsibility would have done him good..." At this point she dabbed her eyes with the corner of her apron "But lord knows what'll happen to him now..." She stood then, bobbing a little, her weight first on one foot and then on the other and I wondered whether she was perhaps impatient to be away but then she suddenly gushed, "Oh sir, I do hope you don't mind my asking and I wouldn't want to speak out of turn, but has anyone ever told you you look like..."

"Yes, yes. It has been mentioned," Pierre interrupted swiftly. "So this room... It is recently decorated?" Sophia looked abashed and colour rose to her face. I looked at Pierre out of the corner of my eye, wondering who it was he resembled. Meanwhile, Sophia stammered a little over her reply.

"Oh yes sir, well no sir. I mean, not recently so's it would make a difference to your investigation sir. And not so's to make big changes. The master likes things to keep what's it he says 'a degree of consistency' sir. Says too much changing around of this and that gives him a headache sir. Says a house should reflect the Good Lord's creation. Ordered and predictable."

"Ah yes," agreed Pierre with a nod of his head. "Order it is very important, no. It gives a feeling of security."

"That's what the master says, yes," she agreed, then she paused and looked at us in a confiding manner. "I don't remind him of the Good Lord's thunderstorms or the Good Lord's earthquakes," she said with a chuckle and again her face was transformed by the laughter upon it. "Anyway sirs, I am forgetting myself. Can I get you a cup of tea before you ask your questions? Cook has been baking too - there are fresh teacakes, still warm if you'd like sir."

At the mention of food, I became aware of the presence of my breakfast. I did not think it would be needing company for some while yet, but Pierre evidently possessed a different constitution from my own.

"That is wonderful," he said with enthusiasm. "Yes, if you please. The English tea and the English tea cakes. This will do us well, a second breakfast for us little how you say... hobbits!" He laughed joyfully and clapped his hands as Sophia bustled out of the room. "Have you read this new thing?" he asked me, "Oh but wait! Bien sûr you have not or if you have you have no memory of it! Oh!" he said delightedly. "I have envy of you! All these wonderful things, these books, these hobbits!" He laughed and I confess I did not know what to say to him. No light went on in my mind this time. I was saved from further awkwardness however by the return of Sophia, this time with another woman, an older, quieter woman, who followed her into the room carrying a laden tea tray. Sophia went to a nest of tables in the corner and brought the largest one over to where we sat. Onto this the tray was placed and the other woman turned to leave.

"No, no!" exclaimed Pierre. "Please, stay, stay. We will ask the questions of madam also." The woman turned back towards him, looking uncertain as to whether he had meant her. "Oui! Yes!" he said. "Please. Stay. Have the seat," he gestured to the chairs opposite where we sat. "Please, both of you. We can chat, yes?" The two women sat and Pierre smiled at the older woman.

"And you must be the cook, yes?" he said. She nodded.

"Ellie sir," she said. Her voice was soft as dust.

"And you make these wonderful teacakes," he added. "Very good, very good." He paused to demonstrate his appreciation by taking a bite. When he had finished chewing, he said, "So your master likes to keep his affairs in order. I wonder how he was affected by this event." He said it lightly, conversationally, but I saw how his eyes were bright, watching the faces of the cook and the housekeeper. They looked back at him, the cook placidly, almost I thought as though she was in her turn appraising him, the housekeeper with signs of confusion. Predictably it was she who answered.

"Affected him, sir? I'm not sure as I know what you mean. I mean, of course he was upset by it - who wouldn't be sir, but upset with the master is, well to be honest sir, it just makes him more busy sir if you know what I mean."

"Indeed?" Pierre uttered the word slowly, his eyes narrowed. Then he said, "So has Mr Beresford has been more busy recently?"

Sophia nodded.

"In what way more busy?" he asked.

"Well sir," the housekeeper blustered, "He always has a project you know. It's a new investment or a new direction for the company sir. A new way to expand. He's in cars you know," she added, and the importance with which she seemed to imbue this statement impressed me despite the fact that I had no understanding of its implications.

"Cars. Indeed..." Pierre responded with appropriate feeling. "Ah this is a good place to be these days in England is it not, in cars?"

"Oh yes sir," responded Sophia with enthusiasm. "The master is doing ever so well you know." Here, a small sound indicated that Ellie, the cook, was about to speak.

"Mr Beresford is a good business man," she said. "He has worked hard and has done well. We are pleased to play our small part in supporting him."

"Indeed," Pierre said again, turning his attention to the cook. "And from what I can see madam, you do it admirably." The cook inclined her head in acknowledgement of his praise. "And Master James?" Pierre said, still addressing the cook. "Is he following in his father's footsteps?" The cook met his gaze.

"Master James is of a different mould," she said in her soft voice. "He takes after his poor mother. He is just a boy and has little desire to grow up as yet. He is not heartless and yet I wonder whether this escape from an early marriage might have come as a relief to him."

Pierre held her gaze for a moment and nodded slowly but said nothing.

At that moment, there was the sound of gravel crunching outside and we turned, all of us at the same moment, to look through the large window. A young woman stood there searching in her bag, presumably for her house keys, and beside her a small boy whose piping voice could be heard, though not distinctly, through the glass of the window.

"That's Millie home with the little master Beresford," said Sophia, rising to her feet. "Will you be wanting to speak to her too sir?" Pierre spread his hands in a welcoming gesture.

"Mais oui! Why not?" he replied "Please, and the little boy too. His name?"

"Alfie sir," she said. "The little love." She squirmed a moment - a little wriggle of pleasure I thought - at the mention of the child then left the room just as we heard the front door open and the high pitched voice became clearer.

"So I said everything would be alright because my daddy can mend anything can't he?" No answer to this confident appraisal was forthcoming however, as at this moment all other sounds were drowned out by the clucking and cooing of Sophia who was presumably wrapping the object of her noise in an embrace as the next, slightly less distinct words to reach us were, "You're squashing my nose Sophia! You're squashing my nose!" and a few moments later, the door was pushed open and Sophia re-entered the room with an affectionately proprietorial hand on the shoulder of the youngest master Beresford.

Pierre rose to his feet as they entered.

"Ah! Master Alfred," he said, solemnly extending his right hand to the level of the boy's own.

Alfie shook it and looked confidently up into Pierre's face. "I am Pierre and this is my assistant, Sam."

I nodded in what I hoped was a friendly manner although to tell you the truth I felt more nervous in the presence of this child than I had at any point I could previously remember, which admittedly was not saying much as my memory did not contain many 'points' at all.

"Hello!" the boy replied. "Are you car people? You don't look like car people."

"Indeed, you have the skills of a detective!" exclaimed Pierre. "We are not, as you say, 'car people'. We are in fact car-less people although not," he added, "care-less people I hope. Now. Will you join us for our second breakfast, Master Beresford? We have the tea cakes made by Miss Ellie. Very good indeed." And Alfie having seated himself on a chair, with some difficulty as the seat was higher than his legs were long, Pierre passed him a teacake. Sophia gasped and scuttled off returning a few moments later with another little china plate.

"The master won't want crumbs!" she said warmly.

As little Alfred munched on his teacake, the door opened once more and the young woman whom we had observed through the window came into the room. She had taken off her coat and hat and was dressed simply in a dark skirt and a cream jumper. She really did look very young, her dark hair held tidily back from her face and her large dark eyes moving enquiringly from person to person. When she saw Pierre, I saw a flicker of something in her expression that could have been recognition, which was followed immediately by a slight frown. Her thoughts, whatever they were, were interrupted by the shrill voice of her young charge.

"Susan!" he exclaimed. "Susan! I'm having teacake!" Susan smiled at him affectionately and her smile seemed to warm the air of the room. The boy turned to Pierre. "Susan looks after me," he said confidingly. "In the night, I scream and scream and I don't know why, but Susan comes and tells me that everything will be alright and it is alright because Susan says so," he said, confident in his precarious logic.

"Night terrors." It was the soft voice of Ellie, the cook. I had almost forgotten that she was there - she was so quiet and still beside Sophia's bustle and Susan's youthful sparkle. "My own boy had them. Years and years. But they passed. Then, so did he." She looked Pierre full in the face and again I was struck by her forthright expression. "I used to tell him everything was alright too," she said, her voice even softer than before, I thought perhaps so that the child would not hear. "But then one night he slipped away and I realised that all that time I had lied to him." She paused, her eyes still on Pierre's own. "Will there be anything more?" she asked then. "I must be getting on you see."

"I see," Pierre said. "Yes. I see. No. That will be all. I will speak with Susan now." The cook nodded and left the room.

I looked around to see whether anyone else had overheard the brief exchange, but the housekeeper, the nanny and the child were engaged in some sort of guessing game and even now appeared to be thoroughly engrossed in it.

"No! You're both wrong!" the little boy crowed triumphantly. "It was a butterfly!" He clapped his hands and laughed freely and joyfully, an infectious laugh that had everyone else laughing along with him. On hearing our laughter, the attention of the adults was drawn to the fact that the cook had left and that Pierre was waiting to speak to Susan. Sophia rose a little stiffly to her feet from where she had been kneeling on the floor in front of the boy and went to sit again in the chair which she had previously occupied. Susan sat next to Alfie, who had by now finished his teacake and was sitting with his arms on the arms of the chair and his little legs sticking straight out in front of him, surveying his realm.

"Well then," Pierre said jovially. "Here we are. Miss Susan I hope you will not mind if I ask you some questions also. Just one or two and then my assistant and I," he nodded towards myself, "must be on our way."

"Of course sir," Susan replied. Her voice was low and pleasant and somehow well-bred. Pierre smiled.

"Good, good," he said. Then he turned to Alfie. "Do you have a favourite toy Alfred?" he asked. The child nodded.

"Yes!" he said. "My Meccano! I've built a car. Do you want to see?"

"I would like that very much," said Pierre and as the boy jumped down from his chair and left the room, I realised that Pierre had intended all along to induce the boy to leave without making it obvious that this was his aim. I looked at him with admiration as he turned back to Susan. "So it is your job to look after Master Alfred," he said. She nodded.

"Yes sir," she said.

"And you like your job?" he asked.

"Yes sir," she repeated, her eyes alight with enthusiasm.

"And these night terrors?" continued Pierre. "They started when?"

"Six months ago now sir," she replied promptly. "He was two and a half. I remember because the first time was the night of my birthday. I hadn't been here long at the time."

"And apart from these he is a happy little boy, no?" Pierre stated rather than asked.

"Oh yes," she confirmed.

"And how do you cope with the night terrors yourself?" Pierre asked. "Are they disturbing to you?" She hesitated.

"Not now sir. At first I worried that there might be something really wrong but now I know it's nothing serious, I just hold him and tell him that everything is alright. It doesn't usually last long after that." Pierre nodded thoughtfully.

"And is everything alright?" he asked. "Is everything really alright? Do you never feel terror yourself? Do you worry about the future, Miss Susan?"

I looked at my companion curiously. He was looking intently at Susan, studying her face. I followed his gaze. To her credit, she did not appear in the least startled by the question but considered it carefully and then said, "Yes, sometimes. But I hope that things really will be alright, sir."

"And this thing? This murder of a young woman? Is this thing alright?"

She met his gaze and said simply, her voice calm, "I believe that justice will be done."

Pierre met this statement with a silent, inscrutable stare. After what felt like an inappropriately long pause, he smiled and said, "Thank you Miss Susan. You have been very helpful."

She smiled at him - a serene smile I thought - and said, "I'm glad I could help."

Just then, we became aware of a banging and scuffling at the door. Sophia went to open it and in came Alfie, proudly carrying a Meccano model of a car. He beamed at Pierre.

"I've got it!" he said, holding the toy like a trophy. "When daddy finishes playing golf he's going to help me make it even better!" Pierre leaned forward to examine the model.

"A fine car," he said. "I think it will go far." At this the child beamed happily and began to drive it around the floor. Sophia swooped down on him like a falcon.

"Not on the carpet!" she exclaimed. "Take it to the nursery, there's a dear." And flinging a happy 'goodbye' over his shoulder at us, the 'dear' did as he was told.

We left the house cushioned by warm bluster from Sophia, her assurances that we were welcome back at any time and her hopes for our success in the investigation. When we left the drive, Pierre indicated that we should turn left instead of going back the way we had come.

We walked for a few minutes without talking. I could not say what thoughts occupied Pierre's mind, but my own were in turmoil. I was confused and, truth be told, a little despondent. It was Pierre who spoke first.

"Tell me what you are thinking," he said. "I am eager to learn how a fresh mind, uncluttered by memories and preconceptions, will perceive these conversations. Tell me what you make of these people, of these answers."

We walked a few more paces as I tried to order my thoughts enough to put them into words. It was a struggle to know where to start. In the end, I started with the thing that loomed largest in my mind.

"Someone is dead," I said slowly. "Killed." I paused as my brain wrestled with words and wondered how to express what I was thinking. "So a life that was well and had a future is now ended. The world continues without her." I paused again, then said, "And death, this thing that stops all other things, is coming to us all..." Here I glanced at Pierre to try to ascertain whether he understood what I was trying to say. It was difficult to tell. He was walking as before, a measured pace, and looking straight ahead. "These people, they know this. They know of the murder - in fact your arrival must bring it more clearly into focus - and yet they are preoccupied not with the spectre of mortality but with keeping a tidy house, with reassuring each other that everything is alright, with play." I stopped again. I was not sure that this was the kind of observation for which Pierre had hoped. "I'm just not sure I understand," I finished lamely. "I'm sorry." I glanced again at my companion but he was still walking, his expression the same as ever. After perhaps half a minute, when I was beginning to wonder whether he had forgotten me, he stopped and turned to me with a smile.

"This is very good!" he said.

"It is?" I did not know what else to say.

"It is," he echoed. "Very good. Your uncluttered mind sees things very clearly. People respond in different ways to the entrance of death into their lives. Their reactions tell us much about them. Your reaction says much about you, also."

I felt at a loss to know what to say in reply to this, but felt that I should say something and so I said, "So, have you found out anything that will help with your investigation?" He looked at me with a sparkle in his eyes.

"I am here merely to restore order. Order is very important."

"You said that when you were talking to Sophia," I agreed. "But I'm not sure what you mean. In what way is order important?"

He looked at me in a curious manner, then he smiled again and said, "The whole universe depends on order and mankind is obsessed with it. Take society, for example. Society is simply a way of bringing meaning to what would otherwise be chaos. Anarchy. You see, Sam, throughout history men have believed that the order of society corresponds to an underlying order built into the universe itself. It is that order that I am here to restore."

I looked at him. Despite my impaired memory and my inability to make sense of the simplest thing, I wondered whether perhaps he was being just a little bit presumptuous with this claim, but I said nothing of it and instead mumbled, "It is a privilege to see how you work. I will watch you with great interest."

"That is good," he said, nodding vigorously. "Very good, because a girl has been murdered, and these things bring disorder and unhappiness. People hold firmly to their belief that things are 'in order' - that life is 'as it should be.' For many people, the murder of someone so young has the effect of undermining that faith. We must work to restore it." I did not reply immediately but something gnawed at the back of my mind. A discomfort. An anger I suppose. After a moment it burst from me and I am afraid my tone was less civil than it might have been.

"Even if that faith is misplaced?" My companion seemed not in the least ruffled by my confrontational tone. His reply was quite mild.

"Ah. You mean like the child who is told that everything will be alright, when ultimately, you are thinking, everything will not be alright?"

"Well, yes, perhaps."

"You think perhaps it would be better to let the child cry?"

"Well, no, I didn't… So we lie to our children?" I slumped. My head was hurting. I did not know what I meant. "I'm merely saying that people apparently say things without knowing why. Or that they say things because they feel they ought to be true - that these are the things they ought to say." To my surprise, Pierre beamed at me.

"You see," he said triumphantly. "You are my ideal assistant, Sam Roden. You have forgotten everything, which includes everything that is of no importance. This means we can talk about the things that really are important without all those unimportant things getting in the way. Now answer me this. When the adult says to the child, 'Don't worry; everything is going to be alright,' do they feel as though they are lying? Or do they feel as though deep down, in ways they do not understand, there is order, and that things can be alright, in a very real sense?"

"I would imagine they feel as though they are telling the truth."

"They do. And this is very important. And now it is time for lunch." He paused and I tried again to order my thoughts, this time including space for lunch. I wondered whether I was proving my own need for order over anarchy but did not have long to consider it because Pierre was speaking again. "Later," he instructed me, "when you are back at the guest house, be sure to tell Elizabeth what we have been discussing. I think she will find it very interesting."

Chapter 5

Lunch was pleasantly quiet. Pierre did not ignore me, but he did not talk as much as he had at breakfast. I assumed that he was thinking about the investigation and the conversations we had had at the Beresford house. This suited me. I was also thinking about the conversations. Why, I wondered, did grown up people play? Golf, the boy had said. Playing golf. Why did they spend time building up companies, decorating houses? If death was coming to us all, why were people so... I sought for a word. Blithe. Carefree. Even when they were not free of trouble, they were somehow carefree. Or, I corrected myself, if they were not carefree, their cares were linked with their projects and not with their mortality. Thinking about small things whilst heading towards the eternal abyss. I thought of Ellie the cook. Perhaps, I thought, there were some exceptions. Her eyes seemed to look constantly into the breach. I looked at Pierre and wondered what he was thinking. Restoring order. I couldn't see how our conversations could lead to answers for him. I said as much. He finished what he was chewing and then said, "I am observing people. The way they behave, the way they speak, the way their eyes shift when a question is asked. Sometimes, Sam, the way to find a killer is simply to dig. You see?"

I was not at all sure that I did see, but I said nothing and we finished our lunch with our own thoughts for company.

After lunch, we went to a newsagent's so that Pierre could buy a paper. I listened with interest as he made small talk with the elderly man behind the counter. I have to say that my impaired mind would not have been capable of such a thing. The conversation, such as it was, touched on Pierre's investigation.

"Hanging's too good for 'im," the man declared. "Still, justice will be done. I'm a great believer in that, sir. Justice will be done." I glanced at Pierre and saw that he was looking intently at the man. 'Observing people' he had said. I realised that this was his constant occupation. In fact, I thought, he was observing me just as surely as he was observing anybody.

After taking our leave of the newsagent, we turned right out of the shop. We were in the middle of the village's main street that ran parallel to the seafront but was set back from it by perhaps half a mile. On this street, as well as the private houses, was the tea shop that also served lunches and where we had eaten ours, the newsagents, a post office and a grocer's shop. We walked along it for a minute or two and then turned right into a side street that climbed steeply and soon left the houses and shops behind as it gave way to grassy meadows on either side. At the top of the hill, the meadow on the left hand side insinuated itself between the cracks in a dry stone wall and slunk through to the other side where it gradually took on the form of a church yard. Grave stones sloped and leaned into each other like tired old men, graves overgrown, the wind soughing through them sadly. Beyond it, the church, all grey stone and squat tower added to the feeling of desolation that sighed around the place. I was not sure what gave it such an atmosphere. The building was well kept and although some of the graves, especially the oldest ones nearer the meadow were very unkempt, the ground around the church itself was neat and cared for. I supposed it was the graves themselves that made me feel as I did, full of death as they were. I looked away from it and over the meadow on the other side of the road. When we arrived at the top of the hill, we paused outside the church gate and Pierre pointed in the direction in which I was looking.

"That house there," he said. "The one with the red roof. That is where we are going." I followed his gaze and saw that sure enough, about three hundred feet from the road at the end of a rough driveway was a fairly large, pleasant looking bungalow that might once have been attached to a farm. Now however it was surrounded by neat gardens. It had a welcoming aspect to it, quite different from the gloominess of the church. Its red roof was supported by whitewashed walls and clematis - which at the time I could not have named - climbed over the front door. Pierre began to walk towards it and I followed willingly. It was a most inviting place.

The uneven, earthen driveway brought us to a neat fence that surrounded the house and gardens. A low wooden gate opened onto a stepping-stone path that led across well tended grass and between neat flowerbeds to the red front door. In front of the door, forming a shallow archway was a wooden trellis, over which the clematis grew, spreading beyond it onto the wall. Pierre looked back over his shoulder at me and smiled.

"It is a pleasant place this, is it not?" he said and, without waiting for a reply, added, "This is where Sylvia Rosen lives, the best friend of Mary Downing. You will like her I think. We are here to see how she is doing. She is very sad to lose her friend." He turned back to the door and knocked upon it gently.

I wondered whether perhaps it was too gentle a knock - I had only just heard it myself, standing as I was right beside the door - but almost immediately I heard a rustling and shuffling from its far side and it swung open to reveal a young, golden haired woman. Her face was pale but swollen and blotchy and I realised that she had been crying. She saw Pierre first and smiled a weak, watery smile.

"Pierre!" she said, "I'm so glad you came back. I was hoping you would." I felt my eyebrows rise. So Pierre had already paid a visit to Sylvia. I wondered when he had done so. He smiled at the girl.

"I wanted to see how you were feeling now," he said, "and I wanted my assistant here" he gestured towards me "Sam Roden, to meet you. We are asking questions you see. Finding out what there is to be found. We have come to see how you are feeling." She looked at me then and nodded but seemed unable to muster up another smile. Her whole countenance was one of sadness and fragility, as though she might simply break apart at any moment. I saw her chin crumple and her lip quiver and I wondered whether she might do so immediately, but she held herself together and stepped aside to allow us in.

We found ourselves in a stone-floored hallway that led off to left and right of the front door. Opposite us and a little to the left was another hallway, leading off at right angles to the first. To the right and left of that were doors, one of which was open and showed a comfortable sitting room beyond it with a fire crackling in the hearth. At the far ends of the hallway, to the left was a kitchen - I could see brightly polished copper, pristine work surfaces and bundles of herbs hanging from the ceiling - and to the right, the passage way curved around and presumably ran some way towards the back of the house, parallel with the second hallway that we could see from where we stood. Sylvia indicated that we should follow her into the sitting room. We did so and she invited us to sit on a large, comfortable settee whilst she went to get some tea.

When she had left the room, Pierre said in a low voice, "Sylvia lives here alone. She is an orphan. When she was sixteen her parents were killed - an accident - and they left her this house and lots and lots of money. She has a gardener and a housekeeper and until recently a best friend to share it all with. Now, she has only the house and the money, the gardener and the housekeeper. She is sad and alone, little Sylvia. I do not know what we will do with her. She is not one of mine but I try to help a bit."

I nodded, trying to imagine how Sylvia must feel. Sad and alone, Pierre said and 'not one of his'. A strange way of putting it, I thought, but already I was getting used to his rather foreign turns of phrase. He was right, after all. She was not his daughter or his sister, not his friend, not his responsibility. Not 'one of' anyone's really. A bit like me, but she must have felt it more because she remembered what it was to have those people and so her loss was greater than mine.

As I was thinking these things, Sylvia came back into the room carrying a tray on which was a teapot and three cups and saucers. She placed them carefully on the low table in front of the settee and poured tea into the cups before handing us one each. Then, she sat down in a large, comfortable looking armchair and observed us over her own cup. We sat in silence for a minute or two, drinking the hot tea and then Pierre replaced his cup on its saucer and said, "How are you today my dear?"

Sylvia did not reply immediately. She did not stammer or start or try to reply hastily out of politeness. She had instead an air about her of one who has suffered and has learned that haste is not helpful. She leant forward and put her cup and saucer on the table, before sitting back in her chair and returning Pierre's solicitous gaze.

"I miss her." The statement was so simple and yet far from being bald, it was laden, saturated with feeling. As she said it, it was as though I was tilted to peer into another abyss. It was similar to what I had felt earlier that morning, with my first remembrance of death. It was the feeling of separation, of grief, of loss. I looked at her and saw that her eyes were once again full of tears. I wondered for a moment how many tears a body could cry before it dried out. She spoke again.

"I don't know how I will ever live without her. She was not just my dearest friend; she was my only friend. When my parents died, she..." Sylvia's voice trembled away. She swallowed then continued, "She had just lost her father. She understood. We did everything together. We had other people of course. But not other people like each other." She looked at Pierre. "We loved each other," she said simply and again, I felt as though a few simple words had opened something infinite in my soul. Love. I had no memory of loving or of being loved, but suddenly I felt drenched in it. I knew what love was and I craved it.

"It is not good to be alone," Pierre said. I looked at him, wondering whether he had somehow understood my thoughts, but I realised that he was replying to Sylvia, who nodded and then shook her head.

"But I am, Pierre. I am quite alone," she said.

"Not quite perhaps," Pierre said gently. "I am here am I not?"

"You are," she said. "But you will go away again and then I will be alone." She looked straight at him. "I miss her," she said again and there seemed very little to be said in response.

A few more minutes passed during which Sylvia picked up her cup and resumed drinking her tea. After a little while, she looked up at me.

"I'm sorry Mr Roden," she said. "I'm afraid I have not been very good company - I can't have made a very good first impression." She smiled a sad smile and I returned it, gently I hope.

"Please don't apologise. It must be terribly difficult for you just now, when everything is so raw. Perhaps after a few weeks or months have passed it will become easier for you to bear." The smile faded from her face and she frowned slightly, a look that I couldn't read, almost as though what I had said made no sense to her. I realised that I may have spoken too lightly. Perhaps this sort of loss was not something from which one recovered. "I'm sorry," I said. "I'm afraid I'm not good with words." She smiled that same sad smile again and then, seeing that our cups were empty, she offered us more tea. Pierre glanced towards the window and Sylvia and I followed his gaze. Although it was not yet evening, the light was beginning to fade and Pierre shook his head.

"I am afraid we must be on our way," he said. "But we will see you again. Do not despair little one, everything will be alright." I looked at Sylvia and saw that she was somehow reassured by this. It made me wonder again how and why people said such things and meant them and were encouraged by them, surrounded as they were by mortality. However I said nothing; it was not the right time. Sylvia came to the door with us and stood there, watching as we made our way along the path. As he shut the gate, Pierre turned and waved to her and I looked back too and smiled. She returned the smile and gave a little wave before stepping back into the house and closing the door.

We walked a little way in silence, down the rough driveway, back onto the road from where we could see the shadows in the churchyard lengthening, turning their faces towards the east as though in anticipation of tomorrow, before being swallowed up in night. As we turned left and began to walk back down the hill towards the main street, Pierre said, "Little Sylvia. She is a nice girl."

I agreed that she did indeed seem 'nice' and added that it seemed unfair that such a person should suffer so much loss when other, less 'nice' people were allowed an easy life. Pierre looked at me. "This is a much raised point with people," he said thoughtfully. "It is my opinion that it seems this way because of the tunnels."

"The tunnels?"

"Yes, like the Sergeant you see. All people have the tunnel vision. It is like looking down the length of a very big telescope. You see one thing very clearly, very close up, but the rest of the picture is out of sight. Now, if only you could take away the tunnel vision, you would see that the picture is much, much bigger and makes perfect sense." I looked at him. He had a serene expression on his face, as though for him, the 'tunnels' as he called them were no obstacle at all. I shook my head.

"Well it seems to me that Sylvia Rosen's tunnel is particularly dark," I said. For a few minutes, so were my thoughts.

My oppressive feelings lifted a little as we turned right onto the main street. Shops were shutting now and people were gathering in small groups as they bumped into acquaintances on the way home, or met up with friends on the way to somewhere else. There was an atmosphere of equanimity - almost of complacency - here in the village. Sylvia Rosen's sadness seemed to be far off now, as though caught up in the cloudy sky. Still I held it, like one holds onto the end of a kite string. I looked curiously at the people we passed, wondering what they thought, how they felt, who they were. At the corner of the street, outside the grocer's shop which was still open though it would not be for long, a group of people were standing in a relaxed group. They were mainly young adults. Two of them, a man and a woman, were hand in hand, whilst several others lounged against the wall or sat on the crates outside the shop, laughing and joking together. As we approached, I saw that at their centre was a much older man, who suddenly burst into song.

"Show me the way to go home," he sang as he staggered about in an exaggerated way whilst the young people laughed with him and a few of them joined in the singing. I stared at them as we got closer, watched their faces, listened to their laughter and their singing. They were relaxed, comfortable. They didn't seem to notice the two of us as we passed by. As we turned the corner to the left and headed back towards the seafront road, the blithe, effervescent voices faded behind us. As the last bubbles of their song burst and we were once more alone I said, "How do they feel safe enough to relax, to laugh and joke and sing? Ever since I remembered what death is, I have had it on my mind. We are not safe from it, from the effects of it - from loss and pain and oblivion. No one is safe from it and yet they hardly seem to think of it at all. Look at them! All these people we've spoken to; The Beresford servants, the man in the newsagents, those people there... They're facing death every day and yet they pursue projects, play games, sing songs, love, hate, hope, judge and joke!" Pierre looked at me.

"You are right," he said simply. "They feel that they are safe. They feel that they are immortal. Perhaps this is not a terrible delusion but a fundamental truth. Have you considered this possibility? The possibility that people generally behave as though they are immortal because deep down, they know that this is the case?" I frowned irritably.

"Mary Downing died," I replied, my tone curt and clipped. "So did Sylvia Rosen's parents. So will I."

Pierre paused then, "Yes... and no," he said. I shrugged, exasperated at what I considered to be his contrary evasion of the issue. We walked the rest of the way in silence.

The last of the afternoon light was being swallowed by the autumn evening when we arrived back at the guesthouse. Pierre announced slightly pompously that he was going to his room to 'consider the day's work' and when we reached the first landing he took his leave of me. Left alone I looked around and out of the window at the sea. The tide had withdrawn and the large swathe of sand had a look of desolation about it, lying naked under the grey-clouded sky. I shivered and turned to go up the stairs to my own room. As I reached out to take the door handle, my previous vision returned of a different room beyond it. Pink chintzy wallpaper and Victorian furniture. The vision was so strong that I found myself taking a deep breath as I turned the handle to open the door, half expecting to find it as I imagined, but of course it was not. All was as I had left it that morning, except that there were signs of tidying having been done. I hung up my coat and hat and wondered what I should do next. I remembered that in the lounge downstairs there was a bookcase full of books and I decided that reading some of them might be a good way to pass the evening. Perhaps they might even help to jog my memory a little. Having decided this, I did not procrastinate but went downstairs. I browsed the books on the shelves and before long came to one whose title seemed somehow familiar.

"The Hobbit," I read aloud, softly. I took it from the shelf. The Hobbit. For a moment I could not remember where I had heard the word before, but then it came to me and I laughed to myself. Tea cakes. I smiled and decided that this was the book I had to read. I looked around the room wondering which chair to sit on but as I did so, I remembered the long view of the garden from the breakfast room window. I suddenly felt a strong urge to sit there again, reading my book looking out at trees and shrubs and the well tended lawn. Still holding the book, I left the lounge and went again into the hallway. I had my hand on the handle of the breakfast room door when suddenly Elizabeth emerged from the adjacent door that led to the back of the house. My presence must have startled her for she let out a little scream when she saw me there and it took her a moment to recover her composure. I apologised profusely for the discomfort I had caused and explained my intention to read my book in the breakfast room. I complimented her on her beautiful garden and said that I should like very much to have that view beside me as I read. For a moment I thought I may have said something amiss - perhaps it was not the done thing to read books in the breakfast room - for she gave me what seemed to be a most peculiar look, but she rallied immediately and I realised that she was probably still recovering from the shock of seeing me there. It occurred to me again how little I knew of reading people's expressions and again I was thankful that it was Pierre and not myself who relied on being able to do this.

Elizabeth showed me into the breakfast room. It was not yet completely dark, but it would not be long before the garden would be swallowed up in shadow and Elizabeth apologised.

"I am afraid you will not have much of a view to look at after all," she said. "Should I draw the curtains?"

I said that I would prefer to have the curtains open; an outside light illuminated the trees and shrubs and it would be pleasant to glance up at it from my book. She showed me a lamp in the corner of the room next to the window and said that I might switch it on if it helped me to read more easily. She indicated the armchair beside the window, the one I had noticed that morning, and invited me to sit there and make myself comfortable, which I did. After she had left the room, I began to read. I was soon engrossed in the tale, which was easy to read and undemanding. In fact, when Elizabeth reappeared about an hour and a half later, I was surprised to discover that I was already about a third of the way through the book. I looked up as she entered the room and it felt as though I was surfacing from a deep ocean or from a dream as the world of Middle Earth fell away to be replaced by the breakfast room and the night-shrouded garden. I smiled in greeting and although Elizabeth did not meet my eye, I thought she smiled too. She crossed to the window beside which I was seated and now, the darkness pressing more closely against the glass, she made to draw the curtains. At the last moment, she must have remembered our earlier exchange because she looked at me and said, "Should I draw them now?"

I said that she should if she wished and so she did. The room became smaller now that it had lost its reflection, and somehow safer. I thought Elizabeth was about to leave the room, but she stopped as though she had remembered something and turned to me instead.

"You were out with Mr Pierre today?" she said. It was not the question I had been expecting, supposing rather that she would ask me about my room or some other such thing. I was nevertheless not entirely surprised by it. Pierre was a curious, eccentric character and if he was investigating the killing of Elizabeth's daughter, well then of course she would be interested in his movements.

"Yes," I replied. "He called me his assistant, but I think I was less 'assisting' than 'observing'." I smiled a little wryly. "And even that I did with a distinct lack of intelligence in the matter." Elizabeth looked at me. She seemed to be trying to place me - to work out who and what I was. I don't mean that I thought she knew who I was. Just that she was interested in what I was thinking. Naturally, I thought. Why wouldn't she be when her daughter was dead and I was, however incompetently, a part of the investigation into the matter. She seemed to confirm my thoughts by coming back across the room and drawing up a second armchair, one I had not previously noticed because it was partly hidden in a tiny alcove on the other side of the window. She sat down on it, far away enough to be appropriate, but close enough to converse easily. At first she didn't say anything and I didn't feel that it was my place to do so either, so we sat a minute or two in silence, the clock tick tocking on the wall. I looked at her. She glanced at me once or twice and I thought she might speak, but each time she looked back at her hands instead, which lay in her lap, her fingers moving ever so slightly over one another. I wondered what must be going on in a mother's mind, contemplating her dead daughter, wondering where to begin talking about her. In the event, Elizabeth did not talk about Mary, but about myself.

"Have you remembered anything more?" she asked at last, her voice low and clear. I shook my head.

"No," I said. "Words, concepts, yes. Those things come back to me all the time. Abstract thoughts and memories. Like what golf is for example," I said wryly. "But nothing personal. Nothing that tells me who I am, where I come from, where I am going, what the meaning of my life might be." I sighed involuntarily as I said this and Elizabeth looked at me, a look in her eyes that I could not read. She sat for a moment then said, "Everyone is like you, Mr Roden. Everyone. Only most people do not realise it."

She looked up a little irritably, as though she was displeased with herself for speaking as she had, or perhaps she was irritable with me. I could not be sure. I remembered what Pierre had said about speaking to Elizabeth about our conversations and decided to do as he suggested.

"I wonder about this," I said in reply to her statement. "Today we spoke to people who seemed very secure in their belief that everything will be alright." I hesitated, wondering what to say next. I decided to begin with the conversation I had had with Pierre after we left the Beresford house. "We went and spoke with Mr Beresford's servants," I began. "They talked about how everything has to be ordered, how Mr Beresford likes things to be tidy, how he plays golf..." I paused and frowned then continued, "How everything will be alright." I looked at Elizabeth. "I found it difficult to understand how in the face of murder, people can hold to these things. How can there be order and security when death stalks so closely? How can a mother tell her child that everything will be alright when it won't be?"

"I used to say that to Mary," Elizabeth said softly.

I hesitated a moment and then said, "I suppose my mother may have said it to me, although I have no memory of it... And look what happened to me," I added, feeling slightly sorry for myself.

I was watching Elizabeth's face as I said this and I saw it change. I supposed that I had been insensitive. Her daughter, after all, had been killed, whilst I had merely... I realised that I had no idea how that sentence should accurately be finished, but reflected that since I was sitting here talking to Elizabeth, whilst Mary lay cold and dead, my plight was almost certainly less serious than Mary's. I apologised for my indiscretion but Elizabeth brushed it aside as though it was of no consequence and I wondered whether there was something else that worried her. After a pause, she said, "Where else did you go?"

I told her about lunch, about the children playing, about the newsagent and his confidence in justice being done. As I told her this, I remembered his words and they puzzled me.

"He said that hanging was too good for the murderer," I said "but then asserted that justice would be done. Perhaps this is just a symptom of my memory loss, but I cannot see how this makes sense. If the murderer is hanged then what further justice can be done? How can he have this confidence?" To my surprise, at this moment, Elizabeth stood up quite suddenly, almost upsetting her chair as she did so.

"Excuse me," she said and without a glance towards me, her hand pressed to her face, swept out of the room. Again I wondered whether I had been insensitive in the things I had said. To the best of my knowledge I had never had a child of my own and could imagine neither this circumstance nor the circumstance of having that child violently taken from me. I thought momentarily about following her and trying to help in some way, but immediately realised that the only possible result of my doing so would be to do more harm than good and so instead, I returned to my book.

It was after midnight when I came to the end of the story and as I closed the book and re-accustomed myself with my surroundings, I was aware of a surreal quality to my thoughts. The tick tock of the clock sounded loud in the quiet house and the shadows created by my lamp took surprising shapes, quite unlike their solid forms. I crossed the room and turned on the main light before going back to my corner and switching off the lamp. Then I left the room in darkness, shutting the door behind me. As quietly as I could I crept along the hallway and into the lounge where I replaced the book on the shelf, then I ascended the stairs. The clouds had thinned and through a break in their mass the moon burst, turning the landings to silver and lighting my way to bed. There had been no supper left for me that evening but I did not feel hungry after the surplus of food I had consumed earlier in the day. I supposed that in the emotion of the moment, Elizabeth must have forgotten it. It did not upset me in the least and it was not long before I fell asleep.

Chapter 6

The following morning I once again joined Pierre for breakfast. He seemed to take it for granted that I would do so and that we would again spend the day together, I taking the role of his assistant. I found it difficult to imagine what assistance I might be providing, but he insisted that my 'empty mind' as he called it was very valuable. As I still had nothing better to do, I met him in the hallway, ready for another day of 'observing people'.

I felt more confident today and more comfortable. It was less blustery than the day before and we were able to talk more easily in the face of the sea breezes. As we crossed the road from the guesthouse, I told Pierre that I had found and read the book to which he had referred yesterday.

"Ah!" He turned to me, his eyes alight. "So you are friends with the little hobbits now, yes? This is good. Very good!" He actually clapped his hands as he finished speaking and gave a little laugh. Then, in a confidential, excited tone, he added, "When we get back to the guest house this afternoon, I will give you another book to read. A sneak preview if you will. It is to be published next year but I have one of the unofficial copies. I met you see with the writer of this other book. Another investigation. There are lots of these investigations. Always busy. Lions and witches and wardrobes. Wonderful. Wonderful!" He clapped his hands and I looked at him curiously. From what I had seen of people in the last day or so, he really was most unusually eccentric. "Come with me later to my room and I will give it to you," he said. "It is in my case."

"Thank you," I said. "I will."

We continued to walk. I asked where we were going today and was told that we were going to the school to speak with the school mistress.

"I have questions to ask," Pierre said. "We will observe." I nodded and mumbled something affirmative, although I really had no idea where these questions and observations might be leading.

We walked up a hill, around the back of the cliff that turned the road away from the sea. Towards the top of the hill was the school. It was a small building for a school; significantly smaller than the Beresford house.

"A village school," Pierre said. "One class, fifty children, three teachers. A community you see. Here we are." With these words, we turned into the school gate and were thrown into the midst of the 'community'. The children were playing in the yard, their shrill, excited voices caught up to the sky on the breeze. We made our way to the entrance and Pierre held the door open for me to go in. We were in a sort of entrance hall that also served as a corridor between the school's two main rooms. To the left was the classroom, to the right was a dining hall. The lavatories were in a separate block in the yard. We turned right towards the dining hall and on our right, just before the hall, was another door on which was a brass plaque.

"Head Mistress' Office," it announced. Pierre knocked on the door. A voice, slightly severe in tone, answered the knock.

"Enter!" it commanded. We obeyed. A tiny, steel haired lady sat behind a desk facing the door. The desk looked as though it had been made for someone much bigger than she was. She was so small that, seated behind the desk, she almost disappeared completely, with only the shoulders of her tweed jacket showing above it. However, there was something about her that seemed to fill the room. She seemed to extend beyond the tiny body so that as we stood just inside the door, I felt that there was not much room left in which to move forward. The illusion was broken somewhat when the head mistress spoke again. "Mr Massenger," she said. "Mr Roden. I was expecting you. Please sit down."

There were two seats on our side of the desk. We did as we were told, Pierre with a muted 'Thank you Mrs White'. I noticed with interest that for the first time since I had met him, he did not dominate the room in which he sat. I would have smiled at the fact, but under the head mistress' eye, I did not feel at liberty to do so. Instead, both Pierre and I sat meekly in our chairs and I for one did not meet the sapphire blue eyes that observed me. The head teacher spoke again and I was struck by how it was she, not Pierre who took the initiative.

"Well," she said, "I understand you wish to speak with me. So, begin. How may I be of assistance?" She looked from Pierre to myself and back again to Pierre, who rallied himself and recovered something of his usual aplomb.

"Yes, thank you Mrs White," he said. "We - my assistant and myself - are asking the questions of people who might give us the insight into matters of life and death. You see, murder has been committed and the order of things is disgruntled. Disturbed I should say."

"Either word, it seems to me would be quite satisfactory, if not entirely conventional," Mrs White said with some feeling. "Were I Order - and some I am quite sure would insist that I am not terribly far removed from it - I would most certainly be, as you say, 'disgruntled'. So, let me have your questions." Pierre nodded.

"Certainly Madame," he said. "First of all I am wondering about the children of the school. How are they with the news of this bad thing in their little village? Do they continue to play, to work...?" The headmistress considered her answer before replying.

"The children have a deep seated belief in the restoration of order, as you call it," she said. "They are not untouched by what happened, but they are secure in their faith that things will all work out alright. Yes, they play, they work - some of them, sometimes." I glanced at her face as she said this and noticed that although her eyes were as keen and alert as ever, deep down they sparkled with fun "and sometimes," she concluded, "they cry and we tell them that we will take care of them and that everything will be alright." I looked at her sharply as she said this. There was something about the fact that Mrs White was saying it that made it either the most heinous lie, or imbued it with what I can only describe as a sort of divine truth. She caught my look and I squirmed as she turned to me. "You are not convinced of this, Mr Roden," she stated.

"I am not sure how I can be," I said, as firmly as I could. "If murder happens, then surely that is the ultimate proof that everything is not alright." She looked at me thoughtfully and then turned back to Pierre, who was looking around the office as though searching for something.

"Mr Massenger," she said. "There is something you wish to ask." Pierre gestured around the room.

"These children," he said. "The ones who work only sometimes. I have been in school rooms before where a cane - a switch - hangs on the wall. You seem to have no such thing." Mrs White fixed him with her eyes and then, without releasing him, rose to her feet. She walked around the desk so that she stood only a few feet from him. Even now, with us seated and herself standing, she was barely taller than we were and yet the word that came into my brain was 'towered'. She towered in front of him. She was dressed in a smart, well tailored tweed suit over a rather old fashioned, Victorian style white blouse. Her stockinged feet were encased in sensible black shoes. She still did not take her eyes from Pierre's and I noticed with respect that he did not look away. "Mr Massenger," she said again. "I have no need of such a thing." For myself, I was already convinced, but she continued. "My children are no angels, Mr Massenger, but they do what they are told. Which is more," she added, "than can be said for some angels, is it not." She continued to glare at Pierre and I have to say I felt a little sorry for him. Even someone who claims to be employed to restore order to the universe probably does not deserve to be upbraided for the sins of fallen angels. Pierre, however, seemed remarkably unperturbed under her alarming stare. In fact, I thought he actually seemed to be enjoying the exchange.

"Indeed so," he agreed. "And I am quite certain, Madame, that many angels would also do what they were told, were you to tell them to do it. Quite certain."

Mrs White held his gaze a moment longer and then, with what was almost a smile, she nodded sharply and said, "So then, your next question, Mr Massenger." She did not return to sit behind her desk, but to my surprise, perched on the edge of it, her feet swinging a good foot above the floor. Far from making her look less in control, there was something in this action that merely confirmed her authority. Pierre looked at her, admiringly I thought.

"Yes," he replied. "I must ask you about Master James Beresford. You taught him, I believe."

"I most certainly did," she confirmed. "I remember him well as a child." Pierre nodded.

"He did as he was told?" he asked.

"He most certainly did," she replied. "But not as willingly as the many angels to whom you referred," she remarked and this time I was certain I caught a glimpse of a smile.

"Indeed," Pierre nodded. "He was a little... How shall I say it? Wild, was he not?"

"Not wild, Mr Massenger. Wilful. There is a vast difference as I am sure you are aware." Pierre gesticulated in a conciliatory manner.

"Of course, of course," he said. "Quite so. But he was lacking in order himself?"

"James Beresford," said the head mistress, "was absolutely assured in his belief that order would be there when he needed it. He was not, however, keen on being restricted by it."

"So this marriage," said Pierre. "To Mary Downing. Do you think he was happy with it?"

"I think he was happy that it was not yet a fait-a-complis," she replied. "If you are asking me whether I think he was ready to settle down, then I must reply that no, I do not think he was."

"Thank you, Mrs White," said Pierre. "That is very helpful." He paused and I thought that perhaps he had finished asking questions, but then he added, "Did you also teach Mary Downing? Did she attend this school?" The headmistress shook her head.

"No," she replied. "Mary Downing and her mother moved here only three years ago, following the death of Mary's father. Mrs Downing wished to be closer to her family." She smiled. "They are a local family," she explained. "Elizabeth moved away when she married and returned when she was widowed.

Elizabeth," she said, "was one of my pupils. Mary was not."

"The child Elizabeth did as she was told?" Pierre asked.

"Always," replied Mrs White. "Every single time - except one."

"And that one time?"

"A bigger, stronger child was taunting Elizabeth's younger brother, Edward," Mrs White said. "Elizabeth knocked the bigger child down. A professional boxer would not have been ashamed of the blow she dealt." She smiled, a sad, wistful smile. "Neither was Elizabeth," she added. "She was proud and defiant. She bore her punishment stoically, but always maintained that she would do the same thing again. Thankfully, the occasion never again arose whilst she was in my care."

"That is interesting, thank you," Pierre said, nodding his head slowly.

"You are welcome," she said and then, to my not insignificant consternation, turned to me and said, "Mr Roden, I believe you have a question."

Now, my memory might have seemed quite terminally broken and I cannot say that I had the least inkling of my own personal history, but in that moment, I had something closer to it than I had yet experienced. I felt like a small boy in a classroom who had been assuming that the lesson was mainly for the other children and who was now called upon to give account of himself. I started and I am afraid that I may even have scuffled my feet.

"Well, I er..." I stammered, trying to arrange my scattered thoughts. When this had at least partially been achieved I continued, "I do have one question."

"Well," she said, "What is it?"

"You were right when you said that I was not convinced," I said, amazed that my words were advancing in something like an intelligent manner, "about everything being alright. Is this something that you merely say to the children to comfort them? Or do you believe it to be true?"

I suddenly found myself fixed with those unyielding, penetrating eyes. It felt as though she could read my soul. For one illogical moment I wondered whether she could see through me and read who I was. Perhaps, I thought, she might even be able to tell me what she saw. But the moment passed as she said, "I never say anything that I do not believe to be true, Mr Roden."

"But death?" I said, and I admit I may have mumbled slightly, but to her credit, the headmistress did not admonish me for it.

"Death," she said firmly, "is not the end." Her eyes were unwavering as she said, "As we will all find out, some of us sooner than others." She turned swiftly upon Pierre and added, "is that not so, Mr Massenger?"

"Yes, Madame. It is so." She stood up, jumping the short distance to the floor from where she perched on the desk.

"That will be all?" she asked, although it sounded more like a statement than a question.

"For now, yes," said Pierre and he also got to his feet. I followed his example and Mrs White held out her tiny hand for us to shake. Somehow, in spite of her size, I expected a fiercely firm handshake, but although her grip was indeed firm, it was astonishingly gentle and something in my broken mind gave way a little and I was amazed to feel tears pricking the backs of my eyes. We crossed the small room to the door and Mrs White held it open for us.

"I am glad to have had the opportunity to assist you," she said, addressing Pierre. Then she turned to me and said, "Everything will be alright, Mr Roden."

We left the school in silence. I felt quite shaken by the interview but could not put my finger on why this might be. The head mistress' strength of character was certainly formidable, but there was more to it than that. Somehow, it had felt personal. I still did not know who I was, but there was something. Something in Mrs White's manner, in her confidence, in her statements of the impossible, that made me wonder whether I might be able to discover where I was going. If death was not the end, then surely it was worth finding out what might lie beyond it. I did not voice my thoughts to Pierre. They felt too newborn and vulnerable. But I resolved to keep a hold on them myself and to explore the possibility that they might be pieces of the broken puzzle of my mind.

After we left the school, we went down into the village. After a little while of silence, Pierre chatted about this and that but did not allude to the conversation with Mrs White. He always seemed to know when to speak and when on the other hand I was lost in thought and preferred him to stay quiet. I realised again that he was a very skilled reader of people and envied him a little for this. We went to a tea shop and Pierre ordered tea and tea cakes for us.

"The tea cakes they were marvellous yesterday," he said. "I keep thinking, ever since, every time I think of food, of teacakes. So we will have teacakes now again." They were duly brought to the table with a large pot of tea, milk in a small jug and two cups and saucers. Pierre poured milk and tea and, his mouth already full, indicated that I should help myself to the teacakes.

When he had finished his mouthful, he declared them to be good. "Almost as good as the teacakes of Ellie," he said, happily taking a second bite. After a few minutes, the waitress came over.

"Everything alright for you sirs?" she asked.

"Yes, yes," replied Pierre. "Just right. Thank you." Then, as if it was an afterthought, he added, "Do you know Master Beresford, Mademoiselle?" The girl was evidently very taken with being called mademoiselle and she preened a little.

"Well sir, not know him as such. But I see him around. He was supposed to be getting married to that girl what was... You know..." here she became a little flustered, but soon rallied herself "...except I've seen him with someone else. More than one someone else actually," she said. "I have to go to town regular see, for my mam. Sometimes when I'm late coming back, I see him with one or other of his girls. The other ones." She paused and then, perhaps thinking she had said too much, added hurriedly, "Not that I'm saying he didn't love Mary you understand. I mean, he wouldn't hurt her nor nothing I'm sure sir. Just that he weren't the marrying type sir. Not James. I knew him from school see. He never was one to settle down, least not before he was old. Thirty or something." Pierre raised an eyebrow but said nothing for a moment.

"Thank you, Mademoiselle," he said. "You have been very helpful."

"Oh but I haven't got James into trouble have I?" she blustered. "I mean, I didn't mean..."

"Do not worry," Pierre said. "The only person who will get James into trouble is James himself. Now. Perhaps we might have more tea?" He poured more from the pot into our cups, then passed it to the waitress. We drank our tea and then left the shop.

"Now," said Pierre, "we will walk to the top of the cliff." I looked at him. He said nothing else but began to walk briskly in the direction of the hill on which the school was situated. By the time we drew level with the school gates, I was beginning to wish he would slow down, but he showed no signs of doing so and we arrived on the clifftop, Pierre exuding a healthy glow and myself, well let us just say I was breathing rather less easily than usual. I was glad to stand and look out to sea, gradually recovering myself. Pierre allowed me to do so for a few minutes before saying,

"So, what did you make of Mrs White the head mistress?" I suppose I should have expected the question but for some reason it sent my thoughts scattering again and I took a moment to reply.

"She is very impressive," I said, slowly.

"Indeed she is," Pierre agreed. "She is also the first to know what is going on. I did not inform her that we were coming and yet Mrs Agatha White, she knew. She has ears and eyes and friends, I think, who tell her everything she needs to know." He paused, nodding thoughtfully. "A very perceptive woman. Very wise I think."

"So you think she is right in the things she said?" I asked curiously.

"Yes I do," Pierre replied without hesitation. "I think she is right in every particular. And you? Do you not think this?"

"Well..." I said, "I am not certain what to think. I am intrigued by people. By their need for order and for assurance and their deep seated belief that somehow things will be alright. I am amazed that they play until they die, as though they have a parent watching over them, as though they can hold back the inevitable, when quite evidently they are alone and hurtling towards lonely death." I paused, a little taken aback at my own desolate summing up. "And it makes me wonder." I paused.

"Yes?" Pierre encouraged. "What is it you wonder?"

"It makes me wonder whether perhaps they are right. If this is something that they feel simply because it is the truth. If Mrs White believes that everything will be alright, then perhaps there is something bigger and safer than death. After all, this attitude that people have - this pretence that they are immortal - only makes sense if, in fact, even without them realising it, it is not a pretence at all." I shook my head. "I'm sorry," I said. "As I say, I do not know what I think. I am sure you have more pertinent things to think about. I am afraid I am not much of an assistant," I added ruefully.

"Au contraire," Pierre said with feeling. "You are marvellous. Is the sea not beautiful with its little white horses on its grey hills?" And with this, I considered the subject changed.

Chapter 7

For lunch, Pierre insisted with some force that we have fish and chips on the sea front. I confess I did not share his enthusiasm. The clouds were rolling in and the breeze had picked up but my mumbled protestations were met with stubborn determination and nothing would change his mind.

"We are at the English seaside," he said firmly. "When in England, we must do as the English are doing." I pointed out rather lamely that as far as I knew I was English and that I was not 'doing', but he responded that I soon would be. I tried to say that no one else was 'doing' either, but he brushed my arguments aside with flick of his expressive hands and led the way to the fish and chip shop. I was about to follow him through the door when a poster on the board outside caught my eye.

"Pierre!" I gasped. "This picture - It's you!" He came out of the shop and glanced at the poster. He sighed.

"No. It is not me. It is somebody who looks like me. Or I look like him perhaps I should say. This is Clark Gable, the actor. I am not so very like him really."

I sensed his discomfort and said nothing, but I had to disagree. The similarity was striking. I followed Pierre into the shop. He was ordering for both of us. The food was not long in coming and we took it outside and walked the short distance to the sea front where Pierre was adamant we should sit to eat. We found a seat facing the ocean. It had a shelter built over it, but this did nothing at all to alleviate the intensity of the wind that blew directly in at us. I was very pleased that the food was hot. I found it comforting. I was relieved when we had both finished eating, had disposed of the greasy newspapers in which our lunch had been wrapped and were able to walk once more.

"Marvellous, no?" Pierre said enthusiastically. "The English fish and chips. It ought to be terrible food and yet, it is Heaven. In fact, I think when I go home to Heaven, I shall suggest that fish and chips be on the menu." He smiled at me, an open, joyous smile. Despite my chilled bones, I could not help but smile too.

We arrived back at the guest house earlier than on the previous day. The clouds continued to roll in and there was a strange, otherworldly quality to the air. Pierre confidently predicted a thunder storm and I was inclined to believe him. He invited me into his room whilst he got the book he had promised to lend me, then he excused himself saying that he needed some time to think. I went up to my own room, took off my hat and coat and washed my hands which still felt greasy from the fish and chips. Feeling refreshed although still slightly chilled, I went downstairs and hesitated in the hallway. Once again I felt drawn to the breakfast room and the long, peaceful view of the garden. As I stood there, Elizabeth came out of the lounge holding a duster. This time, she was not startled but had evidently heard my approach and had come to see if she could be of assistance.

"Hello Mr Roden," she said, evidently forgetting - or choosing to forget - Pierre's insistence on familiarity. She looked at the book in my hand. "Do you wish to read in the back room again?"

"Yes please," I replied, "If it's no trouble." She said nothing but smiled that small smile of hers and, having put the duster down on the sideboard in the lounge, led the way. Again, she came in with me and this time she switched on the main light.

"A storm is on its way," she said.

"Yes," I agreed. "Pierre said the same." I looked out at the garden, strangely dark for the time of day and as I watched, the first heavy raindrops fell to the ground. Elizabeth shivered slightly and crossed to the hearth where she knelt to light the fire. Having done so, she straightened and turned to me.

"Would you like some tea or coffee while you read?" she asked.

"Yes please," I said without hesitation. I still felt chilled from my prolonged stint on the seafront and the idea of a hot drink was very appealing. "Tea, please," I added. She left the room and I made myself comfortable in the chair beside the window. I had hardly begun reading however when Elizabeth returned with a tray on which was balanced a cup and saucer and a generously large teapot. Seeing that she would have to put the tray down in order to move a table closer to me, I got to my feet and at her instruction, moved a small table that was nestling in the alcove with the other armchair, to a convenient place beside my own. She smiled gratefully and put the tray down upon it. I thanked her and she asked me if there was anything else I needed.

"No," I assured her. "I am quite comfortable thank you." I expected her to leave me then, but instead she hesitated and remained standing where she was. After a moment, she said, "You went along with Mr Pierre again today?" I agreed that I had. "Did you learn anything more?" she asked.

"I'm not certain," I replied after a moment's pause. I did not want to offer empty speculation. "My mind is more taken up with what might be waiting after death than with what happens in the time leading up to it. And yet," I said, "it is this very preoccupation that is impressing upon me the intrinsic value of life. Of any life," I added, perhaps unnecessarily. "I cannot understand how anyone, seeing the fragility and transience of life, would seek to shorten it." Elizabeth stiffened and looked at me. There was a hunted look in her eyes and I reminded myself again that it was her daughter who had been killed. I could not hold her gaze but looked away into the garden.

"What of a killer?" she said. Her voice was soft but there was an underlying aggression to it I thought. "What if there is a person who has him - or her - self taken a life? What then? Does that person deserve to die?" I looked back at her, then again out into the rain washed world.

"I think not," I said. I did not wish to hurt a grief stricken mother, but at the same time I could not lie. "I wonder if such a one needs longer to live in order to learn the value of life and the seriousness of their crime. I don't know. How could I know, me with my impaired brain? But is not the life of a killer also valuable? Can not such a person become good? And if they are also killed, the opportunity for becoming good is taken away. I cannot see how this is the best way." I looked at her and saw the hunted look lingering. She had her hand over her mouth and I thought I saw tears in her eyes. I looked away, then added, "Perhaps I am wrong. What do I know? Perhaps hanging is the only way that justice can be done and yet, the more I see of people, the more I hear of how they think, the more I wonder whether there is more to life and death than what we can see and whether justice belongs with someone bigger than the hangman." As I uttered these last words, there was a brilliant flash of lightning. The lights in the room went out and a tremendous clap of thunder shook the house. There was a huge crash outside in the garden and both of us started and peered out of the window into the gloom. A pile of bricks lay scattered on the previously neat concrete that was now cracked dramatically down the middle. Elizabeth screamed a short, sharp scream.

"The chimney," she said when she had recovered enough to speak. "The lightning must have hit the chimney." She turned and began to sweep towards the door.

"Shall I go outside and check the roof and the place where it has fallen?" I asked, trying to help.

"No!" To my surprise, her response was shrill and sharp. I sat back down in my chair. I felt as though I had been dealt an almost physical blow with that single word. A pain shot through the back of my head and I clasped it instinctively. I wondered whether perhaps Elizabeth had been right in her initial assessment and that I had, in fact received some sort of injury there. She came back to the window and after lighting a gas lamp, drew the curtains closed. She was breathless and agitated.

"There," she said. "Now. You don't have to worry about it. Read your book and I will sort out the house." With this, she left the room. For a minute or two I wondered at her nervousness and whether I had perhaps said something to make things worse. I decided to put it down to grief and shock and the sheer untimely inconvenience of the house being struck by lightning, which after all is adequate reason. I began to read.

As on the previous evening it was late by the time I finished reading. A few hours previously, when I had reached roughly the half way point of the book, I had switched off the gas lamp and returned to my room, where I ate my supper - I had met Elizabeth briefly on the stairs and she had remembered, this evening, to ask me whether I wanted it - and then climbed into bed to finish the book. Now having finished it, I sat up in bed, placed the book on the bedside table and looked around. It was a most surreal feeling somehow, emerging from a fantasy world and adjusting to my physical surroundings. It felt as though there was a point where the two overlapped and nothing was quite real. It was at this 'overlapping' point that I caught sight of the wardrobe. It was not a freestanding wardrobe but was fixed to the wall and I noticed that unlike the other furniture, this was not new but merely painted to match the rest. My mind full as it was of wardrobes and the lions and witches that lurked in their depths, I climbed out of bed and crossed over to it. I could not have said what I expected to find there, but I reached out to touch it and as I did so, the same vision flashed through my mind as had occurred previously on entering the room. The distinctive chintzy wallpaper, the old furniture. I jumped at the image but it passed and I opened the wardrobe door. The cupboard was deep and had two rows of clothing hanging inside it. The first, nearest the door, was my own and beyond that, against the wall was another rail full of coats. No doubt I had some sort of notion of being Narnia bound - the night was still stormy and my head full of stories - and I parted the coats until I touched the wall. The room was full of shadows and at first all I could see was that it was not the white of the rest of the room. But as my eyes grew more accustomed to the darkness, I realised that I was looking at the pink chintzy wallpaper of my vision. The same distinctive pattern. It was not merely similar. It was identical. Hurriedly I withdrew my hand, closed the wardrobe door and turned the tiny key in the lock. I went back to my bed and determined to think on it not at all but to sleep. Which is what I did.

Chapter 8

I awoke feeling quite refreshed. For the first time since I had opened my eyes on the train, I awoke to a slender finger of sunlight caressing my face and the warmth of it made waking feel paradoxically more restful than sleep. I got out of bed and drew the curtains. The sky was not completely clear - in fact a slightly ominous bank of clouds was building on the horizon - but there was enough blue space for the sun to stretch itself and to warm the storm soaked world before breakfast. I followed the sun's example, stretching and yawning and enjoying the sensation of being alive.

"Whatever that means," I said aloud to myself and the empty room. I realised that arriving here as I had with an empty brain, and being catapulted into a situation where death was a natural focus, had made me wonder at the same time about life. I realised, stretching in the glass-magnified sunlight, that I did not believe myself mortal. This realisation came as something of a shock after all my morbid meditations. Yet it did not diminish my growing conviction that every life was sacred and should be treasured and protected. In fact, the opposite was true. I pondered the implications of this as I washed my face. Surely, if I am immortal and if only my body dies when its time comes, then logically, protecting the body and the life it contains is less important than if this physical world is everything there is. And yet, everything within me objected to this logic. Why? I wondered. I was still wondering when I went downstairs for breakfast. Pierre, as usual, was already there.

"Good morning my admirable assistant. And how does this morning find you?" I smiled.

"Well, thank you," I replied. "I feel very much more alive this morning." Pierre looked at me intently.

"Indeed?" he said. "And why do you think this might be?"

"Well," I began. "Firstly the sun is shining. But also, I feel as though..." I paused. I wanted to choose the right words. "It feels as though there is a sun shining in my mind. I am starting to feel warmth and to see light." I hesitated then, realising that perhaps I had overstated my case. "At least," I corrected myself, "There seems to be less darkness there than there was before."

At this point, Elizabeth came in with more coffee and a hot breakfast for each of us and for a few minutes we were quite engrossed in matters of eating and drinking and thanking our hostess. When we had taken the edge off the morning with a few mouthfuls of egg and bacon, Pierre said, "So, this sunshine in your mind. Tell me more; I am curious."

So I repeated to him my train of thought from earlier about immortality and the value of life and then I said, "What do you think? Why is it that if life continues after death, I instinctively feel that it has to be protected even more earnestly *from* death? Why does immortality make the mortal precious?" Pierre took a mouthful of coffee and looked at me, his intelligent eyes seeming to weigh me up.

"Well," he said after a pause, "I think it is for two reasons. Firstly, if there is an immortal soul in a mortal body, then surely to this immortal soul death is anathema - it is something the soul cannot understand and does not wish to know, so it shies away from it. It tries to hold back the inevitable tide because mortality is something alien and terrible." He took some more coffee and I took a breath, realising that I hadn't done so for rather longer than usual. "Secondly," he said, "I think it is an instinctive belief that beyond the death of the body is a reckoning. That people want time to... how do you say it? 'Sort themselves out' before they move on to where perhaps it is too late to do so. You see, if there is immortality, if there is ultimate order, if there is the potential for ultimate hope, then there is something bigger than death, something - someone perhaps - who is holding it in place. It is this someone, I think, who is shunned as the poet Emily Dickinson said, '*like an adversity*.'" I nodded slowly. It felt as though pieces of the puzzle were coming together, but I still could not see the picture it made. I thought of the book I had read the previous night. Somehow it seemed pertinent although I could not quite see why.

"Aslan," I said. Pierre looked up, his eyes sparkling.

"Ah, you read the book!" he exclaimed. "This is good. Is it not good?!" I agreed that it was good. "And Aslan, He is the best! Don't you agree?" He laughed happily.

"Yes," I said. "He is." I laughed with him and the atmosphere seemed to lighten. We finished our breakfast in a kaleidoscope conversation that sparkled with lions and fauns, witches and ogres and triumphant battles where everything turns out alright.

Within the hour, we were once again walking along the sea front, the wind tugging at our hair and our clothing, whisking our words from our mouths and flinging them to the gulls. Despite the wind, it felt very different from the previous days, as the sun was still managing to hold its own against the clouds. Although the day was cold, there was warmth where the sunbeams touched. We laughed as we chatted and held onto our hats. I felt reborn this morning. I felt like running with the wind instead of fighting against it. I felt happy. When we turned away from the sea front, I told Pierre as much and asked him why he thought this might be. He did not answer immediately but seemed to be turning things over in his considerable mind. At last he said, "I think perhaps you are indeed coming alive."

I looked at him, wondering what he meant. He had not finished however and proceeded to explain himself. "You woke up on that train with nothing in your mind," he said. "No emotion to speak of, no spiritual sensibilities, no mental knowledge. Now, all these things are waking up, coming alive if you will. You are, I think, as you yourself said, seeing the light." He said this with a beaming smile that was sunshine in itself and I could not help but reciprocate. We laughed again and although I felt it quite genuinely, I still wondered why.

I realised that we were heading once again to the Beresford house and asked Pierre if that was in fact our destination. He confirmed that it was and said that we were going to speak to Master James. I nodded, although I hoped that Pierre was not assuming James to be guilty based on the evidence I had heard. It seemed flimsy to say the least. As soon as I thought it, I brushed it aside. If anyone was able to judge these things, it was Pierre, not myself.

We crunched across the gravel and arrived at the front door. This time, I looked not at the door but at the picture window that looked out from the drawing room where we had sat the other day. I thought I saw a movement from within and after a moment, I heard the brisk click of approaching footsteps. The latch rattled and the door opened.

"Mr Massenger! Mr Roden!" Sophia greeted us like old friends. "Come in, come in." She led us to the drawing room, throwing small talk over her shoulder like salt. "Make yourselves at home. I'll go and get some tea cakes and a nice pot of tea. Now. You just sit down there. I won't be a minute." She left the room in a whirl of aprons and I sat down. Pierre meanwhile, crossed to the side window and looked out at the garden.

"Ah," he said with a deep sigh. "There is nothing like a peaceful garden, Sam. Nothing beats a garden." He turned to me. "Don't you agree?"

I said that from my limited experience - or at any rate limited remembered experience - of the world, I did agree and told him about how I preferred to sit in the breakfast room to read, for that very reason. He nodded sagely as though I had uttered a profound truth. I smiled to myself. I was beginning to grow fond of his little mannerisms. I realised, with a small start of pleasure, that I had a friend. My smile grew larger and I shared it with him. Sophia came back at that point with the tea tray, cups and saucers, tea pot, teacakes and china plates balanced precariously upon it. Pierre pulled out the appropriate table from the nest with what can only be called a flourish and gave a little bow as Sophia thanked him. He came to sit beside me.

"Now then," Sophia was saying. "There's your teacakes, your tea. Now. Is it more questions you're wanting to ask, Mr Massenger?"

"Yes indeed," Pierre replied, "I wonder if we might speak with Master James today?"

Sophia's face fell a little, whether because she was not required to stay and talk with us, or whether for some other reason I could not tell. She put a brave face on it however and said, with something approaching her usual enthusiasm, "Oh yes of course. He's upstairs now but I'll get him straight away. He'll be with you directly."

And with this, she left the room. We heard her footsteps receding as she climbed the stairs. Whilst we waited for James to join us, we found plenty to interest us on the tea tray and by the time the door reopened, the tea cakes were almost gone and we had poured ourselves each a second cup of tea.

The young man who entered the room did so in a confident, easy manner, but there seemed to be no arrogance or guile about him. He smiled at us and nodded then shut the door and sat down in a chair. He was fairly tall with a pleasant face, a mop of dark hair above - and slightly over - green eyes and a boyish smile. Indeed, I thought, he really was little more than a boy.

"Good morning," he said. "Sophia said you wanted to ask me some questions." He looked from one of us to the other and evidently came, correctly, to the conclusion that it was Pierre who was in charge for he settled upon him.

"Yes, that is true," Pierre said. "I am here to ask questions." He paused and looked keenly at James. I felt a little sorry for the young man, who began to look a little uncomfortable.

"It's about Mary isn't it?" James said.

"About Mary," Pierre agreed. "About love and about remorse. Now. Just tell me truthfully. Did you love Mary?" James looked at Pierre frankly.

"Truthfully?" He said. "I don't know. I was supposed to be marrying her you know. I liked her. We got along. But love her? I don't know. I don't know what love feels like if I'm honest," he said with something that may have been defiance. "She used to talk about all the things we could do when we were married. All about settling down and babies and..." He paused. "I don't know. I didn't feel ready for that. I *don't* feel ready for that."

"Yes, I can see how you might feel that," Pierre said. "So you wanted to be free of her?"

"Well, yes... And no..." said James. "I mean, I didn't want her to go and get herself killed if that's what you mean. But yes, I was starting to wonder whether there might not be some way of getting out of it." Pierre nodded slowly and then said, "Where were you on that night?" James looked startled.

"That night?" he echoed.

"Yes," Pierre said. "On the night on which she was killed. Where were you?" James stared. After a moment he said, "I don't know."

"You don't know?" Pierre said gently. "The person you were to marry is murdered and you cannot remember where you were at the time? I am sure this is not an accurate representation of the facts. Please. Think carefully. Were you at home? At work? Out with friends? Girls perhaps?" James started and got to his feet.

"I don't know!" he said, his voice rising. "I've said I don't know. Maybe I was out. Yes, that's it. I was out with friends." He paused a moment and then seemed to think better of what he had said. "No. Actually I wasn't out with friends. I was out alone. I went into town and had a drink and wandered round for a while. Then I came home." He looked defiantly at Pierre as though daring him to contradict what he had said. Pierre did not rise to the challenge but instead, also got to his feet. I did the same.

"Thank you," he said, a little sadly. "You have been helpful." He turned towards the door and opened it. As we were about to leave, he turned back to James. "I would advise you," he said, "to do a little research. Watch people. See if you can find out what love feels like. Begin by watching mothers with their children." James' voice was soft as he replied.

"My mother died," he said. "She left her child."

"I know," said Pierre simply. "Death is the enemy, James. Not love."

With that, we left the room and Sophia, hearing the door open, came to see us out. As before, she entreated us to come back whenever we liked. Her goodbyes were silenced by the door closing and we crunched across the gravel, back to the road.

We wandered into the village and Pierre bought a newspaper from the same newsagent's, where the elderly man asked how the investigation was coming on. Pierre seemed preoccupied and thoughtful. I wondered whether he was thinking about James, whether perhaps James really had murdered Mary. Pierre told the newsagent nothing of any significance, mumbling vagaries and leaving quickly. I sensed the man's disappointment and perhaps even slight resentment at being denied information. Over lunch, which I was thankful to eat inside today - the sunshine was welcome but it was still chilly - I remembered my experience with the wardrobe the previous night. I wondered that I had not remembered it before. I told Pierre about it and he seemed to listen but his reply made me realise that his mind was still on other things.

"Yes, it is all coming together," he said thoughtfully. With this, he sank into silence again and I decided not to press him but to tell him my story of the some other time when he was less distracted.

When we had finished lunch, we stepped out onto the main street. The day was still bright and the breeze brisk and invigorating. It seemed to rouse Pierre from his meditations a little; he looked at me quite jauntily as he said, "Next stop, The Stuart family." He pressed his hat onto his head and turning right onto the street, began to walk. His sudden vivacity had taken me by surprise and I found myself trotting to catch up with him. I managed to do so within a few steps and asked him who the Stuarts were. "Elizabeth's family, bien sûr," he said, as though I ought to have known it all along. I thought this a little unfair when I did not have even the slightest memory of my own family, let alone of anyone else's. I didn't consider it worthwhile arguing the point however, and instead answered him with another question. "Do they live close by?"

"But of course," Pierre replied. "She moved here for that very reason as you know." After this second implication that I was mentally deficient, a fact of which I certainly had no desire to be so repeatedly reminded, I remained silent. Pierre continued at a brisk pace all the way along the high street. At the end, where the previous day we had turned left around the corner by the greengrocer's, Pierre continued straight on. I thought at first that he was approaching the house that stood on the corner, but at the last moment realised that he was entering an alleyway that I had not previously noticed, between the house and the walled off foot of a grassy hill that rose to our right. I realised that this must form part of the same hill as that over which the church presided. The alleyway was fairly narrow and although I could have walked beside Pierre, I chose instead to fall behind him slightly. I did not like the alleyway; it was dark and oppressive and I shuddered involuntarily. I followed him around a dog leg bend and along a further straight stretch until we had passed beyond the houses and came out onto the edge of some fields. To our left I could see the pathway leading straight back into the little town, but to our right it went only a short distance before reaching a gate in a low fence. Beyond the fence the field continued and the path meandered through it until it reached a large, white washed house with a slate roof. A brook bubbled over stones beyond it and curved around the corner of the house towards us before disappearing into a cleft in the hillside. Three old birches grew at intervals along the brook and a line of washing was strung between two of the trees. This house was not pristine and well tended like Sylvia Rosen's had been, but neither was it shabby. It merely gave the impression of being well-loved, a home that could not remember a time when it was not full of people; a place where the people were more important than the house itself. As we came nearer, a man of about my own age rounded the far corner of the house and called out to us in a good natured, friendly manner. "Hello! Can I help you?"

Pierre raised his hand and called back, "Hello. Mr Stuart? I am Pierre Massenger. This is my assistant Sam Roden. We are coming to see how you are, to talk with you. Perhaps to ask some questions if this is ok?" His voice rose to form the question and I sensed again his ability despite his extreme self confidence, to phrase things sensitively. We were now quite close to the man, who held out his hand to us. We shook it as he replied.

"I am Edward Stuart," he said. "Please, come in. The house is full as usual but if you will excuse the chaos..." He turned and walked the few paces to the dark blue front door. I noticed that the paint was beginning to peel at the bottom corner. He invited us in and called out to announce our arrival. We were standing on a grey stone floor in a long hallway that disappeared around a corner and gave the impression of being the beginning of a maze. A woman's face, possibly that of Edward's wife, appeared around the corner of the hallway.

"I'll get some tea," she called and her face promptly disappeared. I heard her footsteps receding into the maze.

Edward ushered us into a sitting room that apparently also served as a play room, a sewing room and a general living room. An older man was sitting on a chair beside the guarded fire, staring into the flames. Behind him, a large window looked out onto the birch trees and the brook. On the hearthrug a small child of indeterminate gender was playing with a wooden truck. A young woman was reading and an older woman sat darning socks at a wooden table at the other end of the room, where another large window showed the approach to the house. Before anyone had time to say a word, two more small children gusted into the room, ran once around it doing a fine impression of a whirlwind and then disappeared out of the door again. Their voices lingered a moment behind them, flinging laughter back along the corridor before they disappeared and left a quietness more apparent than it had been before.

"Mam, Dad," Edward said, "This is Mr Massenger and Mr..." He looked apologetically at me.

"Roden," I said with a smile. He smiled back.

"Mr Roden," he finished. "I think they've come to ask about..." His voice trailed off and I saw him glance uneasily at the man beside the fire, his expression suddenly thoroughly miserable. "About Mary," he said and then quickly added, "I'll go and help Margaret with the tea," and he hurried away, thankfully

I thought. The man beside the fire did not look up, but at the mention of Mary I saw a spasm of what I can only describe as anguish, pass across his face. It was almost palpable. I imagined I could feel it as a pain in my own heart. At the same moment, the older woman put down her sewing and with a small smile that was quite staggeringly similar to her daughter, Elizabeth's, crossed the room to us, holding out her hands in welcome. She moved them to indicate a rather comfortably worn armchair, the double of the one in which her husband sat, and a more upright one beside it.

"Please, take a seat," she said. "George," she added, turning to her husband, "these gentlemen have come to..."

"Yes, I know. I know," he interrupted her, looking at last in our direction. "To ask about Mary." He stared first at Pierre and then at me. He did not look angry, just very, very sad. "Mary is dead," he said softly. "My little Mary. She was the first you know. Our first grandchild. I love them all of course," he said, "but..." He shrugged, turned back to the fire. Pierre went over to the armchair and sat down opposite him. His wife, Elizabeth's mother, left the room.

"She was very special, Mary," Pierre said gently. The older man nodded. They sat in silence for a few moments and I placed myself as quietly as I could on the other chair, trying not to disturb them. Whilst we were sitting in this way, the woman whose face I had seen in the hallway came into the room with a tea tray. The other young woman, the one who had been reading, came across and moved a small table onto the hearthrug, shooing the small child away as she did so. The two younger women then melted into the background whilst Mrs Stuart reappeared and poured the tea before perching on the arm of her husband's chair.

"Thank you for calling on us, gentlemen," she said. "Elizabeth told us that you were staying with her and that you" she looked at Pierre "are looking into what happened to poor Mary. I am not sure that we can help you with your investigation, but we appreciate you coming." She glanced at her husband, who stirred a little and then looked up. I was struck by a change in his expression. Something dark and slightly dangerous was there that had not been there before.

"I think we can help," he said and his voice had an edge to it. "If you want to know what happened to Mary, ask that young man of hers. James." He swallowed and I saw that his eyes were moist. "Or one of his other girls," he added, almost spitting the words. He looked up at Pierre and a tear trickled down each of his cheeks, thrown several times off course by the deep creases there. "He didn't love my Mary," he said, his voice cracking. "He just wanted to be rid of her. Ask him if you want to know what happened."

Pierre clucked soothingly and waited for Mr Stuart to calm down before he said, "That is one person we have spoken to, yes," he said. "I know you must be angry with the young master Beresford for treating Mary badly. This is understandable. But it does not mean that he is a murderer," he added gently. "It is better for yourself not to hate. It is always better so."

Mrs Stuart patted her husband's arm and held his hand whilst the old man allowed his tears to fall freely now. I think she was attempting to relieve the tension when she turned to me and said, "What do you think, Mr Roden?" I was not at all sure what she meant by the question - I doubt she knew herself - and I felt entirely out of my depth as I found myself repeating what I had said to Sylvia Rosen the other day.

"Perhaps time will heal," I said, realising immediately that it sounded lame and insincere, even before My Stuart's anguished voice cut through my self reproach and added to it.

"Time?" he cried. "Six weeks we've had already and the pain is still as raw as ever. Six weeks! Time will not heal. Only justice will heal."

"Hush, hush," said his wife, soothing him and looking apologetically at me, pleading with her eyes that I forgive him his curt response and say nothing more. I would not have known what to say even had I received permission to speak. My mind was reeling. Six weeks? How could it be six weeks? Had not Mary Beresford been killed only three days ago? Was it not her scream I had heard? I found myself wondering once again how long I had slept for after my walk. Perhaps I had, after all, slept for weeks. Or perhaps I thought, the scream I had heard had not been the cry of a murdered woman but had been something else entirely. Had it ever been confirmed that the scream was significant to the investigation? I tried as best I could to rewind in my head the conversations of the past few days, searching for clues, but they all abandoned me and I was left completely in the dark. Mrs Stuart had turned once more to her husband. "At least we still have Elizabeth," she said. "We still have our six children and all our other grandchildren. There are people who would give anything to have as much." Her husband gripped her hand and wept onto it. Edward appeared in the doorway and exchanged glances with Pierre, who stood up.

"Thank you," he said, "for your hospitality." I followed him out into the hallway and from there through the open front door, where the small child, banished from the hearthrug, was sitting picking the paint off the bottom corner.

"Come on Rosie," said Edward and I was illogically pleased that I would not leave without discovering whether the child was male or female.

"Daddy," she said, holding out her hand to her father and flashing a beaming smile at us. Edward scooped her up and held her close, where she continued to grin. Edward smiled at us around his daughter's head.

"Don't mind father," he said. "He'll be alright."

"Yes," said Pierre.

As we walked back down the path towards the town, we could not help but notice the change in the weather. The clouds had finally won the day and the wind had picked up. It had an edge to it and the grey gloom was oppressive after the bright sunshine of the morning. Without hesitation, we turned towards what for the moment at least, was home. I think we were both relieved to arrive back there, a relief which was consolidated by the first drops of rain falling as we stepped through the front door and into the warmth of the house.

Chapter 9

Having finished two books I was eager to read more and so extend my knowledge of the world and of people. (Although some would argue I am sure that hobbits and talking animals are not representative of people nor Middle Earth and Narnia of the world, with my limited experience at the time, I would have already disagreed. Now, with my infinitely more extensive experience, I would still disagree.) With this in mind, having returned briefly to my room and Pierre having taken his leave as usual, I made my way to the lounge and began to browse the bookshelves. Unlike on my first foraging, nothing jumped out at me so to speak. In fact the books seemed particularly disinclined to jump. I was starting to think that I would select a volume at random, when my attention was caught by a glass fronted cupboard beneath the bookshelves. I crouched down to see whether there might be more books in there to choose from and discovered instead that it contained neatly stacked, flat boxes. On the top of one of the piles was a box whose lid was decorated with black and white chequered squares upon which were black and white discs. 'Draughts,' it proclaimed. I slid open the glass door and removed the box, closing the door when I had done so. I straightened and examined the outside of the box. It was as I was holding the box in front of me that Elizabeth came into the room. She greeted me in a subdued manner and I smiled at her and said that I hoped she had recovered from the shock of yesterday evening. At this, she looked at me sharply but immediately the look was replaced by comprehension and she said that yes, she was quite alright thank you. Then, seeing the box in my hands, she said, "Draughts. Will you be playing a game with Mr Pierre?"

"Pierre is in his room," I replied. "He uses the evenings to think." I looked ruefully at the box. "Anyway, I don't know how to play. It caught my eye, and in the absence of a book doing likewise, I thought I could do worse than take a closer look. It is all a mystery however."

"It is not difficult to learn," Elizabeth said. I am sure that Mr Pierre could teach you."

"But not this evening," I reiterated. Then a thought occurred to me. "Perhaps," I said tentatively, "Perhaps you wouldn't mind showing me how to play?" She looked at me and I could not read the expression on her face. Then she seemed to come to a decision.

"Yes," she said. "I will get us a pot of tea and then I will join you." I smiled enthusiastically.

"Wonderful!" I exclaimed. "I will go into the breakfast room and we can sit beside the window." I saw her hesitate at this and realised that perhaps she would not want to sit so close to the reminder of events that she had found disturbing, but she acquiesced and said that she would join me directly the tea was made.

I went into the breakfast room and switched on the lamps. Then, I pulled out two tables, one for the game and the other for the tea. I arranged the two armchairs either side of the tables and was just stepping back to survey my efforts when Elizabeth arrived with the tray. She smiled as she put it down and then looked at me.

"Thank you, Mr Roden," she said. I returned her smile and reached for the box. She sat down and I did likewise. Then, realising that I had no idea what I was supposed to do, I handed the box to her and watched as she removed the board and the discs and laid them out correctly on the table between us. She quickly explained the moves and the intention of the game and we began to play.

For the first few minutes, I concentrated on my moves and asked her questions about whether there were certain techniques I could learn to improve my game. After this, as I began to be able to play more naturally, I found my mind returning to its habitual musings.

"Here we are," I said, after a little while, "playing a game, giving our attention to it. This is what fascinates me about people, about myself. Why we do the things we do, think the way we think, the way we put aside the fact of our mortality and play games." I paused as I made a move. "And yet," I said, "It does not feel unnatural or ridiculous to do so. It feels as though this is as it should be." Elizabeth looked at me, her hand suspended over the board.

"So?" she said. "What are you saying?" I paused, but only briefly. This had been going around in my head all day and now I was ready to give my answer.

"I am saying that perhaps it feels this way because it is this way. Because there is more than mortality, more than time. Because there is immortality and eternity and when we play, we recognise this." Elizabeth looked away and back to the board. She made her move and then sat back and looked at me.

"Perhaps you are right," she said and looked at me for a long moment. I felt uncomfortable under her scrutiny and studied the board. When I had made my move, she said, "If there is eternity and immortality, is there also judgement? Is that where we are heading as we play?" She said it as though only half to me and half to herself. I looked at her and wondered whether she expected me to reply. As she did not continue, and remembering the assertions of the newsagent, I said, "Perhaps this is why people believe that there will be justice even in a case where hanging is too good for a person." She shuddered at the mention of hanging and I hoped that I had not upset her again. She recovered however and said, "A killer should be hanged. That is the law. Perhaps it is a way to avoid ultimate judgement." I looked at her. Her voice was soft and her eyes had a far away look in them. She seemed suddenly to realise that I was looking at her and blinked.

"Do you think killing is wrong for any reason?" she asked me. I was surprised at the question, but recalled what I had said before - that the more I became convinced that death is not the end, the more I valued life before death. I said as much and then added, "So yes, I do. Surely the taking of a life is never justifiable. It cannot be good to snuff out such a vulnerable thing and to send it where we ourselves dare not go." Elizabeth took a deep breath and sighed it out.

"I will put some music on," she said. "Do you have any preference?" I reminded her that having no memory I was hardly qualified to say and she turned away from me towards what I had taken to be just a cupboard in the corner of the room. She opened the doors and drew out a flat, square package from which in turn she took a round disc.

"Rachmaninov's third piano concerto," she said. "Played by Horovitz. It's a very popular recording." She turned back to the cupboard and lifted the top, revealing a turntable. She placed the disc onto it and at once a crackling began. I looked at her, wondering whether this was meant to happen. From her attitude I assumed it was. After a few seconds, the mystery of the crackling was replaced with another, more profound mystery which I confess that even now I do not claim to understand. An energy, a movement of sound, a stirring and then, the most wonderful, the most transporting melody... Even now, I am not sure I have heard one that exceeds it for beauty, but to my new-born mind, it was almost painfully, unbearably beautiful. I sat spellbound. I did not move, I did not speak. The game lay before me on the table, forgotten.

It was more than half an hour later when the music faded and stopped and I remembered where I was. My face was drenched with tears and I was not in the least ashamed of them. I looked across to Elizabeth, who was watching me with an enigmatic expression. After a pause, during which the record crackled and spat softly, she said, "Music is enough for a lifetime, but a lifetime is not enough for music."

She looked away from me and I thought I saw something like anguish written on her face as it turned and surveyed her garden, still with the broken concrete underneath the fallen chimney. "That is what Rachmaninov, said Mr Roden, and he was right." Then, to my great surprise and discomfort, she buried her face in her hands and wept. Between sobs, I heard her say "I am sorry. I am so sorry. Oh Mr Roden, I am so sorry."

As you can imagine, I was entirely taken aback by this behaviour. My own tears, flowing as they did from the sound of the music, had been soft and refreshing and something of which I had become aware only after the event. These tears of Elizabeth's on the other hand, shook her whole body and it seemed as though her heart would break. I felt completely at a loss. I was thankful, then, when without any intervention from me, her sobs subsided and she sat, quiet and still, wiping her swollen face with her handkerchief.

"I am sorry Sam," she said again, softly and calmly now.

"Do not apologise," I said. "I understand that you are grief-stricken after the loss of your child. It is understandable that you weep." She looked at me, her eyes red and tired.

"I feel so weary," she said. "I have the weight of life and death on my shoulders and in my heart." I did not know how to respond to this but thankfully was saved any awkwardness when Elizabeth rose to her feet and crossed to the record player. She carefully removed the record and replaced it in the cupboard. Then, she turned again to face me. "I will get more tea," she said. "Then we can resume our game." I said that this would be welcome and as she left the room, I relaxed a little.

When she returned, she seemed to have recovered some of her energy. She poured more tea and sat down to play. As she did so, we heard a rumble of thunder and she turned to look out of the window. I could imagine that she was not eager to see another thunder storm, but she said nothing and instead played her move. I followed suit and we played in silence for a while. The rain continued to fall but we did not hear more thunder and as the game progressed, I mentioned to Elizabeth that Pierre and I had spoken with James Beresford earlier that day. She looked up.

"And?" she said. "What did he say?" I paused, wondering whether I should have mentioned it at all but realised that now I had done so I could not keep the conversation from her.

"He could not account for where he was on that night," I said. "I think he is suspected of the killing, although I am not convinced." Then I thought about what Elizabeth's father had said and added, "Although Mr Stuart, your father..." I paused, wondering whether I should have mentioned him but having done so decided I had to continue, "He also suggested we speak to James in order to find out what happened to Mary." As I said this, Elizabeth stood up with some agitation.

"No!" she said heatedly. "He is not guilty. He is a silly boy but he is not guilty of this." She pushed her chair back and paced to the window then back across the room. Returning once more to the window she said, more to herself than to me, "I cannot allow him to hang for this. I cannot add that to my list of crimes." I stared at her, wondering what crimes she could mean, but I saw that she had almost forgotten that I was listening and felt too uneasy to interrupt her thoughts. I cast my mind back over our conversations, wondering momentarily whether what I had assumed was grief was in fact guilt. I shoved the thought aside impatiently. Surely Elizabeth was not guilty of her own daughter's murder. In the moment I thought this, she turned away from the window to face me and at the same time, thunder clapped overhead and lightning tore the sky apart. As on the previous evening, the lights in the room went out, but this time they were replaced by the flickering ruddiness of naked flames beyond the window. We both turned to see what had happened and gasped as we saw that the rest of the chimney had fallen and that this time, something amongst them, a bird's nest perhaps, was burning on the concrete where it lay.

The fire did not last long - the rain extinguished it in a matter of seconds - but the charred and blackened bricks remained as evidence of what had happened. The concrete was now even more comprehensively damaged than before and I reflected that it would need to be taken up entirely and replaced. I looked across at Elizabeth, who leaned against the window, seemingly unaware of my presence, staring out into the drenched darkness. After a short while, she roused herself and stood up.

"I will bring your supper to your room," she said, and with that, she left me, a half finished game on the table and tea going cold in the pot.

Chapter 10

It was with a sense of deep unease that Elizabeth left me sitting beside the uncovered window watching the rain wash the rubble of what had been the chimney and pool in the broken ground. I sat for some time, wondering what I should make of her behaviour. For the first time, I wondered whether there might be a different interpretation of her words, "I'm sorry. Mr Roden, I'm so sorry..." I turned them over in my mind until they began to make me feel quite agitated. Was it possible that she had been apologising not for her tears, but for the fact that she herself had taken a life? Again, I thrust the idea away from me, certain once again that Elizabeth had been grief-stricken for her child. Then another thought sidled into my brain; that one can be both guilty and grief stricken. Thus I sat, the rain drumming a tattoo on the glass, my thoughts dancing to the beat, swinging from one interpretation to the other until eventually, I decided to think about it no longer and to retire to my room. I would wait until my mind was refreshed from sleep and then, in the morning, perhaps I would mention it to Pierre. This latter thought made me feel considerably better. Of all people, Pierre would know what to do.

I found it difficult to stick to my resolution in the silence of my room, with nothing to distract me except my cold supper and hot cocoa. In an attempt to occupy my thoughts in less circular ways, I picked up a book that I had noticed previously on my bedside table, but had not yet read.

"The New Testament," stated its front cover. Then, in smaller print, "The Gideons". As I ate, I opened it and turned to where the main text seemed to start. A list of names - a family tree led into an account of a census and baby born under the most curious circumstances. I soon found myself utterly absorbed. The story was told several times by different witnesses of it. A fascinating story that stirred something deep inside me and would not let me put it down. I continued reading and found that the more I read, the more my questions of the last few days were answered and yet at the same time, further questions raised their heads, making my heart beat faster with anticipation of more answers. By the time I had finished, light was dawning on the horizon and instead of climbing into bed, I got to my feet and crossed to the window. As I did so, the sun rose and today there was no cloud to oppose it. Despite my lack of sleep I felt, perhaps for the first time, truly alive.

Having washed and changed my clothes, I went downstairs. I had not slept a wink and yet I did not feel tired. Perhaps, I thought, the tiredness would hit me later in the day. I went to the breakfast room, where Pierre was sipping coffee and reading his newspaper. As I approached him, he looked up and greeted me.

"Good morning, Sam. Did you spend a good night?" I sat down before answering him, then told him about how I had spent what I indeed considered to have been a good night. I told him about how my questions had been addressed in the book and how suddenly I had so many answers that my questions were multiplying because of them. I could hardly contain my excitement and Pierre, to his credit I thought, did not dismiss what I told him but listened attentively and encouraged me in my telling of it. When Elizabeth came in with the breakfast, I told her, too what I had been reading and she smiled a slow, sad smile and her eyes filled with tears. She left without saying a word. Pierre nodded his head - whether in response to Elizabeth or to some silent, internal train of thought I couldn't tell - and said, "Things are moving along, Sam. Moving along."

I hardly noticed what he said, so full was I of coffee and bacon and the discovery of good things. I thought not at all of the previous evening. Nothing seemed important in the context of everything I had learned. We finished our breakfast and stood up. I asked Pierre whether I should meet him as usual in the lounge and he nodded, then said, as if it were an afterthought, "Sunday. Today is Sunday. We will go to church."

Having said it, he turned and walked away without a backward glance. He seemed preoccupied and I felt a little ashamed of my self absorption. I realised that I had not spoken at all to him of the investigation and with this thought, I remembered Elizabeth and the uncomfortable evening we had spent together. I resolved to speak of it as soon as we were on our way.

I met him a short time later and we left the house. The breeze had shrunk from a monstrous predator to a playful companion and the sunshine was glorious in the clear sky. It was not warm, but it was not cold either and as we walked I found that I was smiling.

We walked along the sea front, sunlight scintillating the crests of the lively breakers, transforming them to dazzling dancers. About half way between the guest house and the police station we turned left between the houses and made our way to the main street, crossed it and turned immediately onto the hill that I remembered from the other day; the one we had climbed to reach Sylvia's house. How it was transformed in the sunshine! The meadows shone as the grass bent before the breeze and the morning light rode upon the curved backs of each blade. In the trees and along the stone wall, birds sang and I saw flowers that in the dark oppression of our previous visit I had not noticed. Delicate purples, pinks and whites with occasional bursts of bright yellow were scattered across the hillside to our left and right and I wondered how I could have been so blind to its beauty on our previous visit. I felt as though the once grey, monochrome world had been washed in rainbows. I took a deep breath, filling my lungs with the sun-drenched morning. It was good to be alive. With this thought, I remembered Sylvia and the Stuarts and the fact that death stalks us all. I remembered too what Pierre had said and what I had been reading; considered the idea that death might not be the end but that life perhaps goes on and grows into more abundant life somewhere beyond the grave. We had by now reached the churchyard - were almost at the church gate - and I stopped walking and gazed across the meadows to Sylvia's house then turned and leaned on the churchyard wall, looking at the gravestones in their various states of repair. I wondered about the bodies beneath them, who they had belonged to, whether those people were in fact dead or whether they lived on somehow in new bodies, invisible to us earth bound souls, in a new and better place. If so, then the natural inclination of people to be happy, to plan, to play, joke and judge became understandable, for surely the knowledge of immortality must be sequestered in the hearts of everyone. I straightened and turned to speak to Pierre about my musings and only then realised that he was not beside me. I looked around and saw that he had gone on ahead of me through the lychgate and was standing on the path leading to the church door, half way between the gate and the church. He was talking to someone; a woman. She had her back to me so that I could not see her face, but despite this it was obvious that she was striking to look at. She was tall; taller than Pierre. Slender, but not fragile-looking. She wore a hat and beneath it light, honey coloured curls escaped onto her blue coat. As I registered these details, she turned towards the church and disappeared into the open porch. Pierre turned in the opposite direction and came towards me with a smile. He was still some ten foot away from me when he raised his voice and said, "My colleague is here! I was surprised to see her. I did not know that she was visiting today. A good surprise to see an old friend, no?" He smiled even more broadly and I smiled back. I could imagine that seeing an old friend would be a pleasant surprise, despite having no memory of such things myself. He leant on the wall beside me and as I had done a few moments earlier, considered the grave stones.

"Do you really think these people are living somewhere?" I asked.

"I do not doubt it for a single second," he said. I looked at him and realised with sudden surprise that neither did I.

We didn't stand there for much longer before more people began to arrive. At first they came in ones and twos, dressed smartly and with a slightly deferential look about them. They walked through the lychgate and up to the porch where, after the first few had entered, newcomers were greeted by the robed vicar. As it drew closer to the time the service was due to begin, family groups began to arrive and the original trickle of people evolved into a steady stream. The deferential air changed to a subdued cheerfulness as friends and acquaintances greeted each other and walked together into the church. The bells were pealing now, a joyful shout to call the community to worship and it seemed as though most people responded positively. The Stuart family arrived, straggling down the road in bundled-together groups of different ages, I saw the newsagent looking unusually pious and the girl from the teashop in her Sunday best. Mrs Agatha White arrived, tiny and perfectly neat, startlingly - radiantly - adorned with smiles with which she greeted everyone she saw. Then the stream thinned to a trickle again and Sylvia Rosen came towards us across the fields. She paused at the gate and looked in our direction. Pierre walked towards her and I followed. We went into the church together.

It was cold inside the building and dark after the bright sunshine outside; it took a few minutes for my eyes to become accustomed to the diminished light. High up above wooden balconies, dusty swathes of pale gold and muted reds washed softly through stained glass and draped themselves like sleepy ghosts over pews and pillars. Old, stone-scented air sighed down the aisles as the congregation murmured to their habitual places and settled, whispering in the pews. The final peal of bells died away and was replaced by a strident chord from the organ. I looked to where the keyboard nestled below prodigious pipes and could not but help smiling at the sight of tiny Mrs White, her eyes reflected in the organist's mirror, somehow managing to wield music from the massive instrument. I was sitting near the back of the church, but I was sure that for a moment our reflected eyes met and she winked.

Sitting and standing and joining in with the liturgy was something entirely new to me, but at the same time it felt comfortable, comforting, like a homecoming. I listened to the readings from the Bible and recognised some of them from what I had read myself the previous night. When the vicar spoke on the day's text, I felt again that same stirring.

"He will swallow up death in victory; and the Lord GOD will wipe away tears from off all faces; and the rebuke of his people shall he take away from off all the earth: for the LORD hath spoken it. And it shall be said in that day, Lo, this is our God; we have waited for him, and he will save us: this is the LORD; we have waited for him, we will be glad and rejoice in his salvation."

It was the most beautiful poetry, yet it was not only this that moved me but something infinitely deeper. It was a recognition of truth.

The service ended and the congregation filed out into the unseasonably warm sunshine to the sound of Mrs Agatha White's music. Pierre was in no hurry to move and so we sat, watching everyone else leaving before we ourselves, Sylvia Rosen with us, stood to join them. It was only now, as I saw the Stuart family again, that I realised that Elizabeth wasn't amongst the worshippers and I asked Pierre whether this was usual for her. I realised as I asked that there was no reason, so far as I knew why he should know the answer to my question. Nevertheless, he had one.

"Elizabeth, I spoke to her this morning briefly in the hallway before you came downstairs. I said that we would be going to church and she said that she would not be coming today. She said she was ill. A headache I think." he looked at me. "I think she is a very troubled lady. Many things trouble her." He held my gaze, nodding his head as he did so and I felt unease roll around my stomach. I looked away for a moment and then said, "She seemed upset yesterday evening when we talked. I wondered whether there was more to it than the death of her daughter." Then, realising that I was highly unqualified to make any such judgements, and also that Sylvia Rosen was listening to what I was saying, added, "But I am sure it must be simply that. It is reason enough to be upset." Pierre nodded again.

"Yes, it is," he said.

We stepped out of the porch into the dappled shade of a yew tree and then out beyond that into the thin autumn sunshine. After the stone-shrouded cool of the church, the air felt balmy and I luxuriated in the warmth that seeped through my clothes and skin and into my heart. I breathed deeply and smiled in spite of myself then, as once again I became aware of Sylvia's presence and her eyes on me, I tempered my smile with sadness out of respect for hers. As I did so, I felt an absurd sort of pride as I realised that I was learning empathy.

As we passed through the clusters of people talking and taking their leave, several of them stopped Pierre to greet him and to ask where Elizabeth was today and whether she was alright. I watched, curious, wondering how a newcomer such as he was - and a transient one at that - had managed to find a niche so quickly in the community. Perhaps, I thought it was his unusual self confidence, together with his sensitivity and capacity to care. I hoped that I might one day learn to be a little like him.

At the gate we said goodbye to Sylvia and turned left onto the road. Almost immediately we took another left turn through a low gate in the wall beyond the church. A path led us to a house that had been hidden from the road, first by the church and then by trees that grew almost completely around it.

"This is the vicarage," Pierre announced. "We have an invitation to drink tea. It is so English is it not?" he said delightedly.

We went through another gate in a low fence that was quite obscured by the trees that grew alongside it and walked up the short path to the vicarage. It was a gabled house of irregular shape. I smiled. It was very like the picture in my mind of the professor's house in The Lion, the Witch and the Wardrobe. I liked it immediately. We did not reach the door before it was opened from the inside by the vicar himself, now without his robes. He greeted us warmly.

"I saw you from the window!" he said, as though this fact itself delighted him. "Welcome, welcome. Come in, please. Now then. Mrs Larkin is in the kitchen making the tea so I will take your hats and coats for you. There we are," he said as we handed over the garments as requested and he hung them on a stand beside the door. "Now, please come through. We are all here. It is good to meet with friends is it not." He paused to draw breath and to lead the way along the hall to the sitting room. I wondered as we went who 'we all' might be, but I did not have to wait long to find out because within moments we were there. It was a comfortably large sitting room furnished with stately, old fashioned chairs and lamps and a long settee. At the far end of the room was a window that looked out onto a tree-shaded garden where a song thrush pecked at a worm in the grass. Sitting on the settee were Mrs Agatha White and the woman with whom Pierre had spoken before the service. His colleague, he had said. I supposed that it must have been she who suggested to the vicar that we were invited to 'drink tea'. As we entered, the two women looked up and smiled and I saw that Pierre's colleague was indeed as striking from the front as she had seemed to be from the back. Her face was strong but feminine and had what I can only describe as a radiance about it, although this was certainly enhanced by the sunlight slanting through the window onto it. Agatha White was also smiling and I thought what a pleasure it was to be here with them.

"Please, take a pew," the vicar said to us, indicating the vacant chairs. "Plenty of room for all of us," he added unnecessarily. We did as he suggested and then he himself sank happily into what was evidently his favourite chair beside the fire, and the one which we had instinctively avoided taking for ourselves. He had hardly settled himself when the door opened again and the housekeeper, Mrs Larkin bustled in with the tea. She was cheerful and not in the least deferential to any of us as she poured tea and chattered quite without purpose, but full of gusto.

"There we go vicar," she said. "Your favourite cup with the chip on it though I can't for the life of me understand why you won't let me throw it away. You've got twenty better ones than that with no chips on them. And a biscuit vicar? There you go. I thought so. Keep your energy up after all that hard work. Nice sermon by the way vicar. Rousing. There you go Mr Massenger. Or is it Mr Roden? I know you must be one or the other. Now then let me see. Mr Roden I'm guessing. Not French looking enough for a French man. And a biscuit? No? Are you sure now? Go on. It won't kill you now will it. And you must be Mr Massenger. No coffee I'm afraid but good English tea we do have. Gallons of it we've got. There and a biscuit? Two? Good. That's what I like to see. A man with a hearty appetite." She drew a breath and laughed heartily before turning to the two women on the sofa. "Now then Agatha. There's your cup of tea. How's your brother now? Doing alright is he? Good. And I know there'll be no convincing you to eat biscuits so I won't even try. There now. Miss Harold. So nice to see you again! And looking lovely as always I must say. Why you haven't been snapped up by a young man by now I really cannot think. A biscuit? Yes. That's good. Right. Now anything else you need vicar or should I go and get on with the dinner? Right you are. Give me a shout if you change your mind now," and with that the room fell quiet and still as she closed the door behind her.

The quietude did not last long, although a certain peace still permeated everything. Pierre was the first to speak.

"So, it was a surprise to see you here Angela," he said, looking at his colleague. "I did not know you would be visiting today." Miss Harold smiled at him.

"Really Pierre?" she said, her eyes twinkling, "I thought nothing got past you." Pierre took a sip of his tea and returned her smile.

"Ah this is true. Very true," he said. "Very little gets as you say past me and yet you did."

"I'm here visiting Agatha. She is an old friend."

"A very old friend," Mrs White rejoined, laughing. "At least in body."

"No no no," Pierre shook his head. "Not so old at all. What is it the Scripture says, 'His flesh shall be fresher than a child's: he shall return to the days of his youth.' You see? A few years extra here won't make any difference." He took another mouthful of tea and I wondered what he was talking about. I felt suddenly as though I was on the outside of a circle - welcome but as yet uninitiated. It made me feel excited rather than disquieted - as though I was on the verge of discovery. Mrs White laughed again.

"That's all very well for you to say. I for one will be glad to get my new body once this one's worn out." She smiled at me then and said, "Mr Roden. How are you getting on now? Are your questions being answered?"

I felt a calm assurance as I replied, "Yes, they are. I understand more than I did." I paused, reflecting that perhaps this gave the wrong impression. "That is to say," I added, "I realise now how little I understood before. It seems more obvious all the time that people are as they are because they know that there is more to life than what they can see. It makes sense."

"He has made everything beautiful in its time. He has also set eternity in the human heart; yet no one can fathom what God has done from beginning to end." said Mrs Agatha White. I looked at her, startled.

"Yes," I said. "That's what I mean exactly. Eternity set in the hearts of people. Yes, that is precisely it!" I smiled. What was it Pierre had said to me before? Things are coming together. It certainly felt that way. As though pieces of a giant puzzle were clicking into place.

In the end, we had lunch with the vicar, Mrs White, Angela Harold and the vicar's cat, Snowball, who was quite the most malevolent snowball imaginable and eyed me suspiciously from his red cushion in the corner, hissing if I returned his stare. In spite of the feline hostility however, it was a most pleasant lunch. For the first time since my train journey, which now seemed a lifetime away, I felt truly at home. The conversation ranged from discussion of the wonderfully changeable weather to good food, to the sermon we had heard, or in the vicar's case delivered, to J.R.R.Tolkien and C.S.Lewis and their marvellous creations. We lingered at the table after we had finished, drawing the conversation out as long as we could. Then, reluctantly I thought, Pierre got to his feet, thanked the vicar and his guests and said that we should be on our way. Obediently I followed his example and a few minutes later, hats and coats retrieved from the stand, we were on our way.

We made our unhurried way down the hill. The sun had crossed the sky and lit the meadows differently now. The colours were deeper, sleepier. There was an orange hue to the fields, the rooftops below us, to the air itself. It was only mid afternoon, but this was the overture to evening. We arrived on the main street, where the shops were shut up safe for the sabbath and turned left. At the end of the road, the church hill to our left and the sea cliffs to our right, we carried straight on between them and entered a park. Herbaceous borders and winding paths divided by green painted railings led us to a duck pond next to a playground where a few of the local children cavorted, watched over by their parents who stood gossiping and small-talking close by. There was a wooden bench beside the duck pond and we sat there like secret agents, the whoops of the children and the quacking of ducks accompanying our conversation, such as it was. To my surprise, Pierre produced from his pocket a bag of dry bread and began to feed the ducks. He offered me some and I followed his example, feeling a kind of cathartic pleasure in the activity. Had we sat here like this on previous days, my mind would have been restless and full of angst-ridden questions about the children playing, the parents chatting, our own enjoyment of such small things. Yet today, my mind was peaceful and calm. The questions I still had - and they were multitudinous - lay down in the knowledge that there would be time and eternity to explore them and discover new questions waiting beyond them. All my questions, those that had seemed to be answered and those that were still to be discovered, seemed now a wonderful world to be explored in the light of an eternal and personal deity, and not a tangled web of confusion as they had previously appeared to be. So we sat and enjoyed the afternoon until the sun began to bleed into the western sky and we made our way along the sea front, back to the guest house and to our separate rooms.

I remembered what Pierre had said about Elizabeth feeling unwell and I decided to avoid giving her extra work and stay in my room rather than going downstairs to read. I took off my outdoor clothes and my neck tie and took out the New Testament. Then I lay on my bed and began to read it for a second time.

I was exactly half way through the sixth chapter of the gospel of John, when there was a knock on the door of my room. I was surprised, not expecting to be disturbed and wondered whether perhaps Elizabeth had made something of a recovery and was bringing supper to my room. I called out, "Come in!" and the door opened only slightly to reveal Pierre's disembodied face peering around its edge.

"I have supper in my room," he said. "You will join me, yes?"

"Thank you!" I said. I had not thought about supper until the knock on the door, being engrossed as I was in my reading, but now that the idea had entered my head it was quick to suggest itself to my stomach. I put down my book and got to my feet. Pierre's face disappeared and I followed it around the door onto the landing where it proved to be still attached to the rest of him. We went down a flight of stairs to Pierre's room. It was bigger than my own and overlooked the garden, not the sea. Beside the window was a table and two chairs and Pierre had set out a quite respectable supper. I wondered how he had managed it, but I was becoming used to his idiosyncrasies and realised that if anyone could produce supper at the drop of a hat, then Pierre was that person. We sat and ate together. Whilst we ate, we discussed the few days that had passed since I arrived; the Beresford household, Mrs Agatha White, Sylvia, the police and Elizabeth's family. Pierre repeated his earlier observation that Elizabeth seemed very troubled. I agreed and added, "The police said that she brought the body of her daughter with her to the station. Did they go back to the alley to find clues to what had happened?"

"They went back but found nothing," he replied. "She was strangled you see. No blood, no weapon."

"So did Mary really die in the alleyway?" I asked. Pierre said nothing but looked at me thoughtfully. When he did speak, he said, "Do you think it was Elizabeth who killed, Sam Roden? Do you consider her capable of murder?"

I looked away from him, uncomfortable at being asked to judge such a thing. Then I remembered something that I had heard read that morning in church and said, "The heart is deceitful above all things, and desperately wicked: who can know it?" Pierre nodded.

"That is very true."

When I went back to my room I did not read any more. I felt a sudden, unexpected surge of tiredness and as soon as I could I climbed into bed and slept soundly til morning.

Chapter 11

Monday morning was not as bright as the previous day had been, but it was not raining and as the clouds scudded across the sky, they were spaced widely enough to see the blue beyond them. I felt refreshed by my long sleep and I washed and dressed quickly before going down to breakfast.

When I arrived at the breakfast room, I was surprised to see that Pierre was not already there and felt illogically awkward at the idea of going in ahead of him. I was saved from wondering what to do by his appearance beside me and we went and sat down together. Elizabeth served breakfast as usual, but I noticed that she looked pale and drawn. Pierre looked at her as she came over to our table.

"How are you feeling this morning Elizabeth?" he asked.

She placed the coffee pot on the table and then said, "My head hurts still but I will manage to cook your breakfast." She gave a shadow of a smile and disappeared in order to do as she said.

We ate breakfast without talking much. I think we were both busy with our own thoughts and Elizabeth's haunted face coming and going discomfited me somewhat. Eventually we finished eating and after the usual five minutes or so, met in the hallway and left the house. We began to walk along the seafront.

"Where are we going this morning?" I asked Pierre.

He did not answer immediately but continued to stare straight in front of him as he walked. Then, he said, "For a walk. Away from the house. We need to give her time." I looked at him and felt my stomach flip inside my belly.

"Time?" I said.

"Yes," he replied. "Time." We walked for a little while in the sunshine. We did not talk much. I considered telling Pierre about Elizabeth, but I had a growing feeling that there was nothing that I could tell him that would be anything he did not already know. When, after perhaps an hour, he said, "It is enough. We will return now," and turned a corner that brought us out into a street near the house, I sensed a certain inevitability, as though something had been set in motion that was now fixed and for which there was no going back. Pierre was silent as we walked. I followed his example in this, even as I followed his directions and we arrived within a few minutes back at the house. "Come," he said now and led me through the door that led to the back of the house. His manner was such that I did not question his action, even in the quietness of my own mind. I knew without a doubt that he was not mistaken. Whatever he was doing, it was the right thing to do. I was merely a witness to the fact.

He led me through the kitchen and into a private sitting room, then through another door and up the back stairs. These were not so grand as the main staircases, but narrower and uncarpeted. Our footsteps knocked against the wood and accompanied us with their drumming as we ascended. At the top of the stairs, we came to a small landing and I realised that we were in the attic of the house, above the guest bedrooms. A single wooden door stood in the small, slope-walled space. Pierre leant backwards and with all his weight behind it, kicked the door next to its handle. I would have been surprised, except for my firm and unwavering conviction that he knew exactly what he was doing. The door flew open, leaving the bolt behind. In the centre of the room beyond, Elizabeth was standing on a stool, a noose hanging beside her head, her hands already upon it to place it around her neck.

"That is enough!" Pierre strode into the room and for a moment there was confusion but somehow, when I next saw clearly, the noose was in his hands and Elizabeth was sitting, not standing on the stool, her arms hugged around herself, tears rolling down her face.

Pierre put the noose down on top of a cupboard behind Elizabeth. Then he squatted down beside her and looked up into her face.

"We will talk when we have sweet tea," he said, taking her hand. "Now. Come with me. Easy, easy. Everything will be alright." He helped her to her feet and slowly, we descended the stairs, Pierre never letting go of Elizabeth's hand. She was shaking badly and I wondered whether she would reach the ground floor without having to be carried. She did so however, and when we reached her sitting room, she managed to cross the room alone to sit in a comfortable armchair that faced into the room, away from the window. Pierre said that he would go and make tea and left the room, leaving me to sit with Elizabeth. There were three more chairs, two at right angles with the window and one opposite Elizabeth, the four chairs forming three sides of a rectangle. I sat opposite her. From there, I could see the sun shining on the garden, the breeze trembling the treetops and turning them silver as they caught the light. I looked at Elizabeth but she did not look at me. Instead, she stared down at her trembling hands and from time to time, a tear splashed down upon them.

Pierre returned quickly with the tea. He had made Elizabeth's in a large bowl-like cup and handed it straight to her.

"You need lots of tea," he said by way of explanation. Then, he gave me a cup and saucer of more usual proportions and kept one for himself. He put the empty tray on a coffee table that stood between the four chairs and sat down on the chair closest to Elizabeth.

"Right," he said when he had sipped his tea and when he had made sure that Elizabeth had done the same. "What is this you were doing? I think you must tell us now in your words." He took another sip of tea and leaned back in his chair, waiting for her reply. She gulped and I could see that she was struggling to contain the tears that continued in spite of her to fall.

"I deserve to die," she said when she had gained some control. "I am a murderer and murderers deserve death." I felt my eyebrows lift, involuntarily. Although I was not completely unprepared for this account of things, the sound of it coming from her lips was still surprising.

"That is true," Pierre agreed and I noticed that he did not seem in the least taken aback. "But this is not the way." He drank some more tea. I noticed that Elizabeth's hands were shaking so much now that her tea spilled slightly onto the arm of the chair. Pierre evidently noticed too, as he reached out and took the cup from her and placed it on the tray. Then, he sat back and said, "You must go to the proper authorities and let the law deal with this. But first," he said, putting his own cup beside Elizabeth's and getting to his feet, "there is something you need to show us, is there not?"

Elizabeth started and her eyes filled with fresh tears.

"I cannot!" she exclaimed, her tone frightened. "Please, not that!" Pierre did not move but looked passively at her.

"It must be," he said. "Look," he gestured towards the window. "There has been help for you already. It will not be a difficult job." She stared back at him, her lips trembling.

"It will be the most difficult job in the world," she said and Pierre did not disagree, but held out his hand for her to take and when she did so, drew her to her feet and held her steady.

"And yet you will do it," he said. "Come, Sam. It is time."

For the first time since Pierre had turned our feet towards home, I wondered what might be about to happen. Up until now, I had felt so assured of Pierre's grasp of the situation that I had questioned nothing nor even, as I realised now with a degree of surprise, wondered about anything. However, as we stood in the sitting room, Pierre supporting Elizabeth with his hand, and as I turned to follow them out of the room, I did wonder. I had an overwhelming sense of foreboding. Perhaps it was Elizabeth's frightened manner, perhaps it was Pierre's solemnity. I do not know. But as I followed them from the room, I again had that sense of inexorability, and the end to which we were moving, I suddenly felt, was one with which I was inextricably involved. We went into the large, tidy kitchen and I noticed, as I hadn't before, that there was a door here that led out into the back garden. Pierre opened it and held it for Elizabeth to go out. Then, still holding onto her, he also went through and held the door open from the other side for me. I followed. I had no choice.

There were two steps down from the kitchen to the concreted area at the top of the garden. Elizabeth stumbled as she descended and I thought she would fall, but Pierre held her steady and in a moment we were all three standing beside the ruined, brick strewn area. The sun had already begun to dry out the puddles and I could see that the damage was really very extensive. I looked from it to Pierre, who I saw was also looking at it. Sensing my eyes upon him, however, he said, "Sam, I think this must be your job. Please. Clear away the rubble and then you must dig a little." I hesitated. I can hardly say what my feelings were at this point. Confusion, certainly. But also anxiety at what I might find beneath the surface. Of course, the word 'corpse' had entered my head. Under the circumstances, how could it not. I did not hesitate for long however. There seemed little point. I knew that I would not - could not - refuse and so, I began. It was not difficult to clear away the rubble, but it was not easy either, watched as I was by Elizabeth in her shaken state and Pierre, imperturbable as ever. When I had cleared away all the bricks and pieces of broken concrete into a heap beside the wall of the house, I straightened. The ground underneath was of soft earth, but it had been pressed down firmly by the concrete and I needed a tool with which to dig. Pierre indicated a large garden spade that had been left leaning against the wall. I went to fetch it.

I let gravity take the spade and then I used my foot to force it further into the soil. I added earth to the rubble beside the wall and it was not long before a sizable heap had accrued. I straightened to give my back a chance to remember its usual shape and as I did so, Pierre said, "Thank you Sam. Now. I must do the rest. Please. Help Elizabeth. Make sure she does not fall." My first thought was that I could not support Elizabeth because of my soiled hands, but Pierre gave me no room for refusal and I swapped places with him. He knelt beside the broken ground and took a small shovel that I supposed he must have found whilst I was digging, although I had not noticed. Carefully, he began to move the soil until what lay beneath it was uncovered. Then without warning, he stepped aside and I saw what was there.

It was indeed a body, but not the body of a young woman. I looked down at the open-eyed face that returned my stare. For a moment, I said nothing. There seemed very little I could say. When I did speak, my voice was hoarse and my words garbled. Any corpse, staring up at me as this one did, might have made me stammer and mumble. But this one was guaranteed to do so. It was not Mary's body, certainly, but I had no doubt that I recognised the face. I had seen it every morning since waking on the train, and several times during each day too. The face was my own.

Chapter 12

"But how? What..?" I fought for words. "I don't understand," I finished lamely.

"Of course you do not understand," Pierre agreed. "Come." He produced a sheet from somewhere - I was too shaken for the moment to question where - and covered the body. This had the effect of releasing me somewhat from its spell. I blinked and looked at him. "Come," he said again. We will go inside. Elizabeth will explain.

We went back into the sitting room and sat as we had before. Elizabeth seemed stronger now. Perhaps it was the relief of having nothing left to hide. Pierre looked from her to myself and smiled.

"There!" he said. "So here we are." I have to say, I thought his attitude rather inappropriately jaunty for the occasion, but considered that this was perhaps because it was not his body we had seen buried beneath concrete in the garden. I said nothing and neither did Elizabeth. "So," Pierre continued. "I will take, as it were, the chair." He turned to Elizabeth.

"Tell us the story please. In your own time." She looked at him, a sort of resignation in her eyes. Then, she began to speak.

"On the night that Mary was killed, I followed her." She looked at us. "I did not make a habit of this you understand. It was just, that night she had left her purse behind. I knew she would need it and when I found it, she had only been gone ten minutes. So I put on my coat and ran after her. I knew where she was going. She always told me. She was going to meet friends that evening because James was busy. Busy with other girls, I thought, but I didn't tell Mary that. I was waiting for the right time and the right time never came." She looked at me, a strange, unreadable look, then at Pierre again. "I came to the alleyway between the field and the shops and as I got closer I heard voices, but I couldn't tell whose they were or what they said, only that it was a confrontation of some sort. So I crept along the alley to where there's that dog leg half way down and I peered around the wall. For a moment, all I saw were two people, a man and a woman. I could see that he was attacking her but couldn't see more than that. I was frightened. I couldn't bring myself to interfere, but neither could I run away. So I hesitated. Then, in a moment, he had killed her. I saw her fall and I saw that it was Mary. The man looked around to see if he had been observed and not seeing me, I suppose he thought he hadn't. But he had. I had seen him. I saw his face. There was no mistaking it - the moon was bright and the light from it fell directly onto his face." She took a deep breath and then she looked straight at me for the first time that day. "You were the man," she said.

She paused then and I stared at her. I had no memory of what she told me and yet something inside me told me that it was true. I lowered my eyes and felt them fill with tears. I blinked them back. She was speaking again.

"I went to Mary," she said. "I held her as she died. Then, I went to the police. I carried Mary in my arms - it wasn't far and I am strong. I told them I had found her in the alley but I did not tell them what I had seen. I felt calm and in control. I wanted it to stay that way. You see, I had a plan."

I sat and listened as Elizabeth told how she looked for the man who had killed Mary, believing that he would return to the scene of his crime. He did so, lingering around the streets nearby, where she found him and lured him to the guesthouse with promises of that which Mary had refused to give. With soft words, she put him at his ease and brought him upstairs to the only unoccupied guestroom. On the landing outside the door, she whispered more promises to him and pushed open the door, inviting him to go in before her. Once he had done so, she picked up a hammer that she had placed there beside the door in readiness for the moment and struck him on the back of the head. The last thing he saw was the pink chintz wallpaper.

Having made sure the man who killed her child was dead, Elizabeth locked the door, first laying his bloodied head on an old coat that could be easily burned. Then, she waited for a time when she would not be seen, collected the body and with only a little difficulty for she is a strong woman, manoeuvred his body down the stairs and buried him in the garden. At that time there was no concrete and the ground was soft. She flattened the earth and the next day asked a local boy, whom she knew to be efficient and obedient but lacking in curiosity, to come and concrete that area. She told him that she needed a change after the loss of her daughter. Then she had the bedroom redecorated, the same excuses being given and believed.

Elizabeth told us all this and then said, "So here I was, entirely justified as I thought in my actions and carrying on quite happily with my life, except for the constant pain of loss, for I missed Mary every single day. And then," she said looking at me again, "you turned up. You with the dead man's face and no memory and all your great pronouncements about life and death and judgement and eternity." She paused and looked away. "Of course I was surprised - shocked. I wondered whether you were the dead man's twin brother. Or even whether I had killed the wrong twin.

That is why I asked you about your family when you first arrived. Then I wondered whether somehow the man I killed had not really been dead and had somehow managed to get away. That did not make sense, but neither did any of the alternatives. Sometimes I thought you were the same man, come back to haunt me. Sometimes I thought you were God's way of punishing me - of telling me that I was wrong. Sometimes," she said with a little, rueful smile, "I thought I was going mad. I still don't know which one it is," she added. "But this morning I realised that my actions hadn't been justified after all. I realised that you, whoever you are, were right when you said those things. I didn't know what else to do, so I did what I did." She paused and looked at Pierre sadly. "Except I didn't, because you arrived and stopped me.

Chapter 13

We sat for a moment, the only sound the ticking of the clock. I felt confused, unreal, as though I was dreaming and as though in a moment I would surely wake up and perhaps then I would remember who I was and all of this - the past few days and the past few hours - would disappear with the dawn of a new day. We continued to sit and I knew that this would not happen. Somehow, impossibly, Elizabeth's story was true. Yet I could not see past my confusion to make any sense of it. Indeed, from what I could tell, there was no sense to be had. Elizabeth was looking at Pierre and I turned my eyes towards him too, for I realised that if there was an explanation then it was he who would provide it.

We looked at him for a long minute, him gazing from one to the other of us, seemingly waiting for the right moment to speak. Presumably it arrived, for at the end of the minute he cleared his throat and began.

"So, I must come clean," he said and for a split second I wondered whether he too had hideous crimes to confess but I quickly realised this was not the case. "I am not a detective. I never claimed to be a detective," he continued as if in his own defence. "I never claimed to be investigating the murder of Mary Downing. I never claimed anything. But people are very impressionable and I," he said, drawing himself up in his chair, "I impressed them." He paused, looking from Elizabeth to myself and back to Elizabeth. "I knew who killed Mary. I knew from the start. I saw it too," he said. Elizabeth gasped and her eyes opened wide but she said nothing. We were both waiting to hear what he would say next. He turned to me. "That scream you heard," he said. "That first night that you were here. It was not a murder. It was children playing. It was what you call a red herring. It sounded dreadful, yes, but then children playing can sound dreadful. Just ask Mrs Agatha White." He chuckled to himself and again I thought his behaviour slightly inappropriate for the occasion. Still, I reflected, if he had known these things all along, perhaps there was no difference to him if he laughed now or yesterday or tomorrow. I looked at him as he stopped chuckling and looked seriously at us again. "So," he said. "I am not a detective. No. I am an angel." I saw Elizabeth's incredulous expression and thought it must reflect my own. For the first time since he started talking, he was interrupted. It was Elizabeth who said it but it might equally have been me.

"An angel?!" she said. Her tone was a mixture of incomprehension, disbelief and ridicule. For once I was certain that I had interpreted her emotions perfectly, simply because I felt the exact same things myself. Pierre however was unfazed.

"Yes, yes!" he said. "I am your guardian angel. Both of you. This is not uncommon for two people to have the same guardian angel. In fact lots of people do. But for one of those people to kill another one of those people... This is not good. It makes me feel bad. It becomes my business; I have to put it right." He stopped, looked at us, then, "So here I am," he said.

We looked at each other, Pierre relaxed, at ease, happier I thought than I had seen him before. Elizabeth and myself quite the opposite. Neither of us yet understood what he meant.

"Put it right?" echoed Elizabeth.

"How?" I asked.

"Simply this," he replied. "I have helped to show you the value of life, the imperfection of mortality and the fact that there is a rightness to be attained. You have felt it, you have read it" - here he nodded towards me - "and now you are free to act on it."

All this time, my brain was trying to nudge me; trying to draw my attention to something. Now, it succeeded.

"But," I said, "I'm dead. I am *dead*, aren't I? That was my body out there in the ground."

"Yes," said Pierre. "But you are also alive as you can see. You have this new body and a little more time to find out what is truly important. That time is almost through. But that is good because you have found out I think. Is this not so?"

"Yes," I said simply and suddenly I knew it to be true. I smiled. For the second time that day, with no sense of irony, I felt truly alive. "I feel like Edmund," I said. "In the Narnia story."

"That is a very good way to feel," said Pierre seriously. Then he turned to Elizabeth.

"And you," he said. "You were unrepentant. You needed to know that what you did was wrong. This was tricky. My plan might not have worked. But it did work!" He said with a wide smile. "Now, you are free to do the right thing." She nodded.

"Yes," she said, as I had done. Pierre sat back in his chair and beamed at us.

"And now," he said with a clap of his hands, "more tea I think." And off he went to make it, leaving myself with my murderer and my murderer with the murderer of her daughter. Our eyes met and from what I could make out through my tears, I think she returned my smile.

Chapter 14

Pierre returned with the tea quicker than I would have thought possible. I remembered the shovel and the sheet and looked at him with dawning comprehension. An angel. I supposed an angel could take just as long as he liked to make tea and what is more, could pluck a shovel or a sheet or anything else he cared to think of from thin air. He put the tray down on the table and handed us each a full cup. Then he sat in his place and surveyed us.

My thoughts fluctuated from an assurance of ultimate well being to a crushing sense of guilt and anguish at what I had been told I had done. I wished I could at least remember it so that I could express remorse. I tried to say as much to Pierre and to Elizabeth. I remembered her tears of the previous evening and realised now that they were for me. "I'm sorry Sam," she had said. Now, I wanted to do similarly.

"Well then," Pierre said when I had finished saying how I was feeling. "This is the next step. I will give you back your memory." He paused and then said with a smile, "But first, finish your tea."

I drank my tea, I confess, slower than I usually would. Although I had said that I wanted to remember, there was part of me that recoiled from the thought of it. The thought that I would know what I had been - that my fingers would know what it was to kill, that my mind would remember what it was to hate and to be hated. But inevitably the moment came. I put down my cup and looked at Pierre.

"I am ready," I said, wondering even as I said it whether it was true.

Pierre got up out of his chair and I made to do likewise but he urged me to stay seated.

"It is better if you are sitting," he said. "It might be startling. Like a blow. Perhaps a bit of a shock," he explained. I did as I was told. I sat and I waited. He put his fingers to my head and said simply, "Remember."

I remembered.

I remembered my childhood, turbulent and traumatic despite having money and education. I remembered my mother, her face bruised, her eyes frightened, trying to hide behind the shield of respectability. I remembered as I grew older, my sisters with similar faces and this time it was I who caused the bruises and the fear. I remembered the shrivelling of my heart, the despair that turned first to hatred and then to indifference to anyone and anything but my own desires. I remembered my name, the name that represented all my self loathing. I heard a groan - a low, animal groan of misery and pain and it was my own voice that made it. I felt Pierre's hand on my arm and heard his voice beside me.

"Everything's going to be alright," he said. "Remember?"

I remembered.

I remembered Mary Downing falling from my murderous hands. I remembered the moonlight and the silence. I remembered returning to the streets a few nights later. I remembered Elizabeth.

I was standing on the second floor landing. The key was in the lock. I was ready for one thing only and it was not death. The door opened and I saw the walls, the pink chintz paper, the antique furniture. I felt the blow but only as one feels a blow in a dream. There was no pain, only darkness - a long tunnel of impenetrable gloom. Then, a gradually intensifying light that first crept then rushed then all of a sudden flooded in upon me.

The angel appeared. He told me that I was about to meet God but that I had time still - that he was here to offer me a last opportunity to hope. He told me that in order to have this opportunity, I had to do what he said. I agreed. First, he said, I must forgive my killer and everyone before her who had hurt me. "Your sins will be forgiven," he said, "if you forgive those who sin against you." Then he told me that there was something else he wanted me to do.

He told me that I would forget who I was. I would be given a new name. Sam Roden, in reference to the Witch of Endor who called up the ghost of Samuel. I would, in a way, be a ghost like he was. He said that he would take care of everything; he would cover all expenses, sort everything out. Again I agreed. He took hold of me and the next thing I knew, we were standing on a station and a train was coming to a standstill beside us. We got on the train and when I was seated, the angel put his fingers to my head.

"Forget," he said, and I fell asleep.

The next thing of which I was aware was the movement of the train. I registered this and as I did so, opened my eyes.

"I remember," I said. I looked at Elizabeth.

"I am sorry," I said and as I said it, I knew that now I would always be Sam. I would never have to return to that old, hated name or my old, hated self. I was free.

"I forgive you," she replied.

Chapter 15

I'm certain that hampered as she was by mortality, the weeks that followed were long and tortuous for Elizabeth. She handed herself in to the police and told them her story, omitting the more recent events that I have related in this account; she had no wish to complicate the trial with musings on insanity. As a result, the case was straightforward. She was found guilty of murder in cold blood and was condemned to death by hanging. Pierre and I attended her trial and visited her in prison and I was interested to see that nobody looked twice at me nor questioned my similar appearance to the murdered man. Pierre dismissed my observation with a wave of his hand.

"People see what they want to see," he said. "Or what they expect to see. They do not expect to see the murderer's victim at her trial or visiting her in her cell." I agreed that he was probably right.

Eventually, on the evening before she was to die, the time came for Elizabeth's last meal. We sat with her although no one noticed us there, only Elizabeth herself. As she ate, we talked. Matters of life and death, of repentance and forgiveness, of eternity. Things about which everyone should talk over dinner with friends, even if they hope that there will be many more such meals to come.

The following morning, we were there again. We watched as the clergyman came to take her last confession, as the hangman came and gently, respectfully, bound her hands and led her through the door to the gallows.

"Pierrepoint," Pierre said. "That gave me the idea for my name."

"You chose your name?" I asked. "Did you not already have a name?"

"But of course I have a name." He hesitated then said, "It is a very... Angelic sounding name." He looked at me, his eyes twinkling. "And not at all French." I frowned, puzzled.

"Why did you have to be French?" I asked.

"Well in the current climate I thought it would be better than being German," he said evasively. "Although there are many, many lovely German people," he added fervently. "I know some of them very well indeed."

"No," I said, trying to keep my own mind, at least, on the subject. "I mean, why couldn't you be English? You were coming to England after all."

"Ah," he said. "Well the thing is, I wanted to be able to say all sorts of true things that coming from an English man would give away too much too soon but from a Frenchman..." He shrugged. "Well, he is foreign. He is allowed to say strange things." He laughed and I smiled at him.

"What's your real name?" I asked.

"Gazardiel," he said.

"Gazardiel," I repeated, turning the word over on my tongue. I looked at him. "Do you mind if I still call you Pierre?" I asked. "I've got used to it." He laughed.

"But of course. And I will still call you Sam. Your new name for your new life." I smiled again and then looked at him curiously.

"So you chose your name because it was French and belonged - in a way - to a hangman," I said. "But Clark Gable?"

He replied slightly defensively, "I liked 'Gone with the Wind.'" This time, I laughed too.

Death came quickly, suddenly, an expected surprise. Pierre held out his hand and she came with us.

We were climbing up a stairway through a golden light. It was the kind of light a mountaineer experiences when climbing a mountain surrounded in white cloud, when the sun is shining brightly above the clouds and he is approaching the place where they open up and abandon him to the blue sky and the imminent peak. The air was clear and easy to breathe. It was no effort to climb.

I do not know how long we climbed, how much time it took or how high we ascended, but the further we went, the more peaceful I felt and it was a peace twinned with an excited anticipation so that although I recognised it as peace, it was unlike any peace I had felt before. It was not simply a numbness or an absence of anxiety. It was an active peace that filled me with joy and propelled me onwards.

The clouds opened out and fell away. We were standing in a garden, bare feet on lush grass. I looked behind and the stairs had vanished. There was only the garden all around. Thick grass grew under beautiful trees and sweet scented shrubs. A stream ran through the garden and animals played on its banks. The air was full of birdsong. I looked at Pierre.

"There is nothing like a garden Sam," he said. "Don't you agree?" I did agree and told him so.

To the left was a wooded grove. We walked through the trees and after awhile they began to grow less dense and we found ourselves at the edge of a plateau, looking out over a valley. I heard Elizabeth gasp and my own mouth fell open as I saw a beautiful world - shining cities and soaring mountains and a river sparkling as it ran out of the largest city and down to the sea, the silver ribbon of which I could make out on the horizon.

Pierre turned to us both and, taking our hands in his, "Welcome home," he said.

So we were home. Home - a place where we can rest and breathe and from where we can see all the pieces of the puzzle and how they fit together. There is a big and beautiful picture written across the eternal sky and everything is going to be alright.

Lightning Source UK Ltd.
Milton Keynes UK
UKOW052340260112

186126UK00001B/10/P